HORSE OF SEVEN MOONS

Horse of Seven Moons

KAREN TASCHEK

UNIVERSITY OF NEW MEXICO PRESS

ALBUQUERQUE

To Lillian,

a modern-day Apache leader

Printed and bound in the United States of America

09 08 07 06 05 1 2 3 4 5

Library of Congress Cataloging-in-Publication Data

Taschek, Karen, 1956–
Horse of seven moons / Karen Taschek.
p. cm.
Summary: In 1881, after sixteen-year-old Bin-daa-dee-nin, an Apache fugitive, prays for help to survive in the mountains of New Mexico, he encounters a unique horse, and the path of his life with that horse crosses the life path of fourteen-year-old Sarah Chilton.
ISBN 0-8263-3215-3 (pbk. : alk. paper)
1. Mescalero Indians—Juvenile fiction.
[1. Mescalero Indians—Fiction. 2. Apache Indians—Fiction.
3. Indians of North America—New Mexico—Fiction.
4. Pinto horse—Fiction. 5. Horses—Fiction.
6. New Mexico—History—1848—Fiction.] I. Title.
PZ7.T211132Ho 2005
[Fic]—dc22
2004024162

DESIGN, COMPOSITION, AND ILLUSTRATION: *Mina Yamashita*

CONTENTS

RATON
GRAND CANYON
MARBLE CANYON
TAOS
LAS VEGAS
SANTA FE
ALBUQUERQUE
ARIZONA
NEW MEXICO
COLORADO RIVER
PRESCOTT
FT. APACHE
PHOENIX
SALT RIVER
SAN CARLOS RESERVATION
WHITE MOUNTAIN
FT. STANTON
HONDO
MESCALERO RESERVATION
GILA RIVER
SILVER CITY
FORT BAYARD
SACRAMENTO MOUNTAINS
FORT CUMMINGS
COOKE'S PEAK
LAS CRUCES
PECOS RIVER
TUCSON
DEMING
EL PASO
CIUDAD JUÁREZ
BISBEE
NOGALES
NOGALES
RÍO GRANDE
GUADALUPE MTS.
RÍO DE LA CONCEPCIÓN
CHIHUAHUA
TRES CASTILLOS MOUNTAINS
GULF OF CALIFORNIA
SONORA
RÍO DE LA SONORA
SIERRA MADRE
CHIHUAHUA
HERMOSILLO
R. YAQUI
GUAYMAS
APACHERÍA

Their land also is full of silver and gold,

neither is there any end of their treasures;

their land is also full of horses,

neither is there any end of their chariots.

—Isaiah 2:7

Part I

AMBUSH

1

The mountain held its secrets. Cold and black, buffeted by a terrible storm that lashed the short mesquite trees and soaked the coarse, pebbly sand, the soaring peak shuddered under thunder. Heavy waterfalls rushed down the mountain's sides, surging over boulders and carving arroyos. The frenzied, wind-whipped trees sprayed cold water droplets in sheets. A bolt of lightning briefly illuminated the flat, rain-slick face of a cliff and two Apache boys struggling to carry something heavy across the ledge in front of it.

"I see a cave—help me bring Nzhų-'a'c-siin inside!" Bin-daa-dee-nin shouted to his brother Yuu-his-kishn over the roar of the wind. The pelting rain ran down his face, and Bin-daa-dee-nin pushed his thick hair out of his eyes. Even with his keen sight he could barely distinguish the darker mouth of the cave through the raging, stormy night.

Bin-daa-dee-nin and Yuu-his-kishn gently carried Nzhų-'a'c-siin into the cave. Bin-daa-dee-nin tried to see the back of the cave but could not. He listened carefully for the rustle of a bear's heavy paws or the scratch of a mountain lion's claws. The cave was silent. *We will be safe here—until next light,* he thought.

"How are you?" Yuu-his-kishn asked Nzhų-'a'c-siin, bending over the other boy. The Apaches had tried to raid a silver miners' wagon for food, and in the struggle one of the miners had shot Nzhų-'a'c-siin. The miners' wagon had crashed into the hillside, and the miners had scattered into the night.

Nzhų-'a'c-siin said nothing.

Bin-daa-dee-nin tried to see Nzhų-'a'c-siin's wound, then his face, but the darkness hid all. Under Bin-daa-dee-nin's hand Nzhų-'a'c-siin's chest was moving very fast. *That is not good,* Bin-daa-dee-nin thought. *But I can do nothing now.* "Light will come soon," he said finally. "We will look at the wound then."

"Light will bring the soldiers to retaliate for our raid—the miners will have reported it at the army post," Yuu-his-kishn said. He sounded tired. "How can we run from them now that Nzhų-'a'c-siin is wounded? I do not even remember how long we have run since Victorio died."

Bin-daa-dee-nin was silent. For a moment he saw the strong, lined face of Victorio, their leader for many moons after the three boys had left the terrible life on the Mescalero Apache reservation, in the white man's year of 1880, to join Victorio's band of Apache warriors. Victorio always knew what to do for his warriors, but Bin-daa-dee-nin did not. "Let us rest," he said, trying to keep the weariness out of his own voice.

"Yes," Yuu-his-kishn agreed. "We'll decide what to do in the morning."

Yuu-his-kishn lay down on the rocky floor of the cave, pillowing his head on his arms. Bin-daa-dee-nin leaned against one of the cold, damp walls, dropping his head to his knees. After a little while Yuu-his-kishn slept, his breathing quiet and steady. Nzhų-'a'c-siin slept too, but he often gasped and jerked.

He needs a blanket, Bin-daa-dee-nin thought, fighting the despair that threatened to seep into his bones as much as the cold. *Winter is over below in the desert, but not yet on this mountain. If our raid had been successful, we would have food and blankets.*

Bin-daa-dee-nin closed his eyes, but he could not sleep. He got up to see if Nzhų-'a'c-siin was still warm and breathing. Apaches were strong, but Bin-daa-dee-nin wasn't sure if anyone could survive such a wound.

If only I had the power to help him, he thought. *But I have never been approached by Power, like some members of the tribe, or given a ceremony to heal.*

Bin-daa-dee-nin sat beside Nzhų-'a'c-siin, letting his face sink into his hands. Nzhų-'a'c-siin, the son of his mother's sister, was his only living relative. "Do not die," Bin-daa-dee-nin whispered. "Not like all the others."

He touched the cold cave floor around him and felt a pitted branch of cholla cactus. The cave had kept it dry from the rain. Crawling across the cave floor, Bin-daa-dee-nin gathered more cholla branches and mesquite leaves and twigs. Then he expertly rubbed the twigs until a small fire glowed near Nzhų-'a'c-siin.

Bin-daa-dee-nin did not look at his brother—he feared to. But perhaps the small fire would comfort him. The soldiers would not ride out in this storm and see it.

The fire's orange light flickered on the slick cave walls. Bin-daa-dee-nin gazed into the black depths of the cave, drawn to them. "Can I pray to the Mountain Gods?" he asked softly. "The Mountain Gods, the protectors of our people." But this mountain was a great distance from White Mountain, the sacred mountain of the Mescalero Apaches. So much had changed since the people had been put on the reservation at Fort Stanton. Would the Mountain Gods hear at all?

Bin-daa-dee-nin stepped cautiously farther into the cave. It seemed to go back a long way. The floor was uneven rock, with small boulders scattered around. When the blackness of the cave enclosed him completely, he dropped to his knees. "Mountain

Gods," he began, "you have Power. Tell me how to heal my brother. Protect us from death. And . . . and let the storm pass quickly." *The storm part of the prayer is foolish,* Nah-kah-told himself. But the thunder and lightning were terrifying—people who got too close to lightning could become sick, and the storm had gone on so long.

The cave was silent. Bin-daa-dee-nin searched desperately, his eyes raking the thick dark, but he could not see any sign. *The Mountain Gods did not hear,* he thought, his shoulders slumping in despair. *We are alone*. Bin-daa-dee-nin rose and walked quickly back to his brothers, longing for their company and the warmth of the small fire.

He lay down on the other side of Nzhų-'a'c-siin and fell into an uneasy sleep.

The tiny fire reared up and blazed fiercely, and the cave filled with a strange, bright light. Five tall, indistinct forms filed in from the back of the cave, four black and one white. They wore masks, and the black shapes had an odd white symbol painted on their backs and chest. The white figure wore a bell that clanged as he moved and seemed to be a clown. The figures all wore a skirt and leggings of buckskin, the old-time clothing of the Mescaleros when deer had been plentiful for skins.

Bin-daa-dee-nin gripped the rocky floor of the cave, fear and great joy surging through him. He knew who they were from stories he'd heard on the reservation—they were the Gáhan, the Mountain Gods.

The Mountain Gods began to dance around the fire, their tall, branched headdresses swaying, thrusting their staves into the flames, and to sing unfamiliar words but soothing. The dance grew faster until the gods were a blur of black and white, light and dark.

With a jerk Bin-daa-dee-nin opened his eyes. The figures were gone, and the night had quieted—the storm had passed. A ragged black cloud, radiant at the edges, slipped over the mountain, and the full moon burst out, drenching the mountain valleys with light. But the cave was completely dark, the last embers of the fire burned to cinders.

Bin-daa-dee-nin leaned against the wall, wiping sweat from his face. His heart was beating fast. That dream had surely been a sign from the gods. *But what should I do?* he wondered. *The gods did not give me a ceremony so that I can bring their power to help.*

He got up and walked over to the opening of the cave. The faint signs of dawn were in the sky—scattered clouds tinted blue and a grayness at the horizon. His perfect sight showed him the vague outlines of the stumpy junipers and mesquite that struggled to grow on this dry mountain and the lumps that were rocks. A quick, cool breeze gusted off the slopes, seeming to usher in the morning. He and his brothers would have to move soon.

As he turned to go back inside, movement below caught his eye. Hope filled him. "A deer?" he whispered. "We will have food!" Slowly, careful to stay downwind, he approached the animal, moving from one tree to the next and staying out of sight. His heavy work boots, issued to him at the reservation, crunched noisily on the ground. He had not worn moccasins since he'd had time to make them, a long time in the past. *I have no weapon but a knife,* he remembered, frustrated.

But the animal was not a deer. To Bin-daa-dee-nin's surprise, a horse slowly crossed the narrow valley, stopping to nibble on the scattered grass between the trees. The horse seemed silhouetted against the heavy full moon, round and white, sinking in the sky.

Bin-daa-dee-nin smiled broadly. *Just what I want!* he thought. *I will be able to travel quickly in hunts and raids, and the horse can help move Nzhų-'a'c-siin.* Pulling his knife from his belt, he quickly cut a long, wiry branch of juniper to use as a rope and approached the horse. *Don't run,* he ordered it silently. *Don't be a wild horse.*

The horse snorted and jerked up its head. Bin-daa-dee-nin stopped.

A breeze lifted the horse's black mane, and its big eyes, black in the faint light, studied him boldly. It was tall, with black-and-white patches and a black tail that swept to the ground. The horse's head, with its small, sensitive ears and broad forehead, tapered to an elegant muzzle, and it had a starburst of white on its black face. Its long, slender legs were poised for flight, but now that the horse had seen him, it did not seem to fear him.

Bin-daa-dee-nin staggered back a step. He had never seen such a splendid horse. *Is this a sign from the gods at last?* he wondered. Summoning his nerve, he walked over to the horse. It tossed its head and looked around at him as he ran his hand over its glossy shoulder. Bin-daa-dee-nin felt his fear diminish. This seemed to be an ordinary horse, though a very fine one.

"Why are you here?" Bin-daa-dee-nin asked. If the horse was a supernatural being, it might talk and tell him what to do in a ceremony to share its power. From living on the reservation, Bin-daa-dee-nin knew that white people regarded such beliefs as foolishness. And of course not every animal brought a message from the gods. But the horse's beauty and sudden appearance could not be denied.

The horse simply continued to look at him, and Bin-daa-dee-nin's hopes that it had power vanished. "Still, you are a horse, and I need you," Bin-daa-dee-nin told the animal. He slipped the juniper branch around the horse's neck and glanced around. The moon was hurrying behind the mountain, bringing in the day. Time to move camp.

"I will call you Moon That Flies," he said. The English words slipped quickly off his tongue, as if they belonged in this strange place.

2

"OUR LUCK HAS CHANGED," Bin-daa-dee-nin said the moment he woke his brothers at first light. "Now we have an excellent horse."

Moon That Flies was looking over the broad rock ledge of their camp. In the sunlight, his black and white patches glittered like ripples in a stream.

"We still have no food," Yuu-his-kishn reminded him, leaning on his elbows. His handsome face, with its high cheekbones, long nose, clear bronze skin, and big black eyes, had attracted many girls in the tribe. Bin-daa-dee-nin was shorter and darker, and his nose had healed crookedly after a wounded elk's antler had broken it. Bin-daa-dee-nin did not much care. He had always valued his hunting, tracking, and horsemanship skills more than his looks.

He peered down at Nzhų-'a'c-siin, who lay on his back. Nzhų-'a'c-siin's face, scarred from its Apache perfection by the smallpox he had suffered on the reservation as a child, was pale, and Bin-daa-dee-nin felt an icy tremor of worry. Although he had seen much death, he did not know for sure if Nzhų-'a'c-siin approached it. But this seemed likely. "Wake up!" Bin-daa-dee-nin said, gently shaking Nzhų-'a'c-siin's shoulder. His eyes fluttered open. "How do you feel?" Bin-daa-dee-nin asked, relieved.

"Not . . . so bad," Nzhų-'a'c-siin said between gasps. "I . . .

don't think I'm bleeding."

Bin-daa-dee-nin knelt beside him. He did not want to look at this wound. He could not treat it, and no matter how bad it was, Nzhų-'a'c-siin would have to travel. But Bin-daa-dee-nin knew it was best to be prepared for whatever was to come. Gently he rolled Nzhų-'a'c-siin onto his side and examined the two bullet holes, the one where the bullet had gone in and the one where it had gone out. The first one was just a round hole, with red around its edges. But the one out Nzhų-'a'c-siin's back was bigger and jagged, with a slow seep of blood staining his shirt. Bin-daa-dee-nin sat back on his heels.

"What do you think?" asked Nzhų-'a'c-siin.

"There is not much bleeding," Bin-daa-dee-nin said. "I think you will heal." That was not exactly a lie. Nzhų-'a'c-siin might have a chance—depending on what fortune threw their way. If he did not have to travel too much, he might be able to heal. The horse could help him move with less effort.

"Come," Bin-daa-dee-nin said to Yuu-his-kishn. "Let's go back to that miners' wagon and see what we can quickly find to eat."

Moon That Flies came to Bin-daa-dee-nin willingly when he stretched out his hand, and Bin-daa-dee-nin slipped the juniper rope back around his neck. The horse could first prove his usefulness by helping to carry back supplies.

Yuu-his-kishn ran down the cliff, jumping from boulder to boulder. Bin-daa-dee-nin followed more slowly, leading the horse. He did not want to ride him yet—the animal might never have been ridden and throw him. Bin-daa-dee-nin was pleased to see that Moon That Flies slid on his haunches, clattered across rocks, and even trotted down smooth stretches. Clearly he was accustomed to mountains.

The wagon was not far from the Apaches' camp. The trip to

the cave had seemed much farther last night, in the rain, with a wounded man.

"Wait," said Bin-daa-dee-nin, crouching behind a huge rock and hoping the horse would be quiet. "Let's see if the miners spent the night here."

But the mountain was completely silent except for the calls of small birds and the whisper as a chipmunk scurried over the sandy ground. The young sun lit the sky in light blue to the east, deepening to dark blue overhead and melting the night's last ice to trickles. Moon That Flies waited patiently behind Bin-daa-dee-nin. He seemed willing to do what was needed.

The boys approached the wagon. Its two front wheels had broken almost in half, and the wagon tilted down at a sharp angle. A sack of flour sagged out the front between the ripped canvas, spilling white powder onto the ground. As he circled the wagon, Bin-daa-dee-nin noted that the mules' harness had been cut. "The miners rode off on the mules," he called to Yuu-his-kishn. "Hurry. They may be back soon, with the soldiers." Bin-daa-dee-nin led the horse to a patch of grass to let him eat, then climbed over the weathered gray boards at the back of the wagon, pushing through the canvas that hung low from the wagon's wrecked skeleton.

In the dim, filtered light Bin-daa-dee-nin glimpsed a huge prize of food, weapons, and clothing. But in the middle of the wagon he also saw—to his horror—a dead man. His body was sprawled to one side across several piles of silver, the neck cocked at an unnatural angle. His open blue eyes stared at Bin-daa-dee-nin, menacing in his bloodless, gray face.

"I will not touch him!" Bin-daa-dee-nin said immediately.

"Don't think I will touch him!" Yuu-his-kishn yelled from behind him.

The two Apaches glared at each other. Finally Bin-daa-dee-nin said, "Let's just go around him, then." That wasn't good either—any kind of close contact with death carried the risk of ghost sickness, where the dead tormented the living—but they had no choice.

Bin-daa-dee-nin squeezed by the dead man, bumping into the useless stacks of silver bars lining the sides of the wagon. The wonderful food surrounding him took his mind off death. He gathered three loaves of heavy, moist bread, a slab of bacon, a small sack of coffee, a bridle for the horse, a length of rope, two shirts, and three rifles and ammunition. He stuffed all the goods but the bridle into a large deerskin sack, one of the few things he had left from his travels with Victorio. The sack was bulging when he finished.

"I have salt and sugar," called Yuu-his-kishn, and Bin-daa-dee-nin's mouth watered at the thought of the feast they would soon prepare.

Don't be greedy, he reminded himself, crawling back out of the wagon and closing his eyes as he went by the dead man. Time to go—the surviving miners would have reached the army fort by now. Even now the miners, with the soldiers, might be returning. Yuu-his-kishn was already out of the wagon, packing his own sack with goods.

To Bin-daa-dee-nin's relief, the horse was right where he'd left him. Moon That Flies raised his black head and whickered. Bin-daa-dee-nin hurried over to him and raised the bridle over his ears. The horse obligingly lowered his head, his soft nose tickling Bin-daa-dee-nin's hand. Moon That Flies seemed to look at him with affection.

Bin-daa-dee-nin shrugged it off. Although it was good that the horse was so used to people, Bin-daa-dee-nin did not let himself care for animals much. He might not have the horse for long—often they were killed in battle, stolen, or even eaten in hard times. Caring for people was difficult enough.

Yuu-his-kishn handed Bin-daa-dee-nin his own deerskin bag, and Bin-daa-dee-nin tied the two bags together, slipping the rope into holes cut into the tops. Then he straddled the horse with them, letting one bag hang on each side. The horse skittered under the unusual weight, but Bin-daa-dee-nin jiggled the reins on the bridle before he could fuss too much. Moon That Flies tossed his black head, but then he settled down to his task of carrying the supplies up the mountain.

Back at camp, Nzhų-'a'c-siin was asleep. "We should eat," Yuu-his-kishn said, sliding the saddlebags off the horse. "I will build a fire."

"No fire," said Bin-daa-dee-nin. "The soldiers will come." He had already decided on the walk back that he would have to wait for bacon and coffee.

"Just a very small one," Yuu-his-kishn said. "The soldiers and miners are slow—and they are probably still eating breakfast at the fort."

Bin-daa-dee-nin hesitated, his hand on his horse's heavy black mane. Yuu-his-kishn was not only older than he was but an initiated warrior. Bin-daa-dee-nin had not had time to be properly initiated, a long process in the Mescalero tribe that involved a boy's slow progression in battle from observer, horse holder, and general helper of the warriors to a fighter, in command of bow and arrows, the spear, and guns. So Yuu-his-kishn still had the traditional right to be the leader of their small band.

But the older boy must not lead them to their death.

"We cannot have even a small fire because of the scouts," Bin-daa-dee-nin said. "They'll see it from a long ways off. And they are not slow." He scowled. Bin-daa-dee-nin knew he and his small band had the most to fear from the Apache scouts who had joined the army—they were expert trackers and tireless.

Yuu-his-kishn's face was expressionless, but Bin-daa-dee-nin could tell from the way he stood, a little slumped, that he was disappointed. "Eat the bread in my bag," Bin-daa-dee-nin said. "Do not wake Nzhų-'a'c-siin—he can eat later. I want to ride this horse and see if he is trained enough to carry Nzhų-'a'c-siin. I'll be back soon."

Before the horse could move, Bin-daa-dee-nin sprang onto his back in a bound, squeezing hard with his calves so that he didn't slip off the horse's sleek back. Moon That Flies pranced a bit but didn't throw him. "Good! He's been ridden before," Bin-daa-dee-nin called. *Always I have longed for a fine horse—now I have one!* he thought. Bin-daa-dee-nin nudged Moon That Flies forward with his heels, and the horse obediently stepped out along the ledge.

This is going well. As Bin-daa-dee-nin guided the horse down the cliff, he tried to come up with a plan for himself and the others. *We will have to stay on this mountain—we won't be able to travel fast. There are many cliffs, and if Nzhų-'a'c-siin and the horse can get up some of them, the soldiers won't be able to follow.* He'd have to think harder about how to escape the Apache scouts, though.

Bin-daa-dee-nin pulled the horse one way, then the other with the reins to see how quickly he would turn. Moon That Flies was a bit slow to turn, especially to the right. Bin-daa-dee-nin circled him around a yucca cactus, bringing him closer to its pointy dark green blades each time. After several circles, Moon That Flies bent his neck into the turns, seeming to understand what was wanted.

"We will work on that," Bin-daa-dee-nin promised, halting the horse. Certainly this was a superb-looking animal, he thought, admiring the cleanly marked, irregular patches of black and white across Moon That Flies' withers. The horse's large, intelligent eyes, set far back on his head, looked back at Bin-daa-dee-nin.

Bin-daa-dee-nin couldn't help grinning. "I could not have

asked for a better horse," he said. He had never had a choice about what horse he rode—most horses belonged to the white people, and he'd had to take what he could get while he'd been with Victorio. That was when he had learned to ride—before then he'd only taken care of the agent's horses at the reservation, cleaning stalls, grooming them, and walking them to cool down when the agent brought them to him steaming, huffing, and lathered after a hard ride.

Bin-daa-dee-nin was Victorio's best horseman by far, often sent ahead to scout, but usually he got only scrubby Mexican ponies to ride, their gaits rough, their minds dull. *This horse is a great gift,* he thought.

Letting his leg brush against the soft needles of a juniper, Bin-daa-dee-nin breathed in the clean, cool scent of the air, heavily tinged with last night's rain. The sky was a sharp blue above the mountain and gently hazy across the wide, pinkish orange plain in front of it. The day was still cold and frosty but would quickly warm. Shoots of wiry grass nudged through the hard soil, the first sign sure sign of spring.

The horse meandered to a ridge, and Bin-daa-dee-nin looked out over the edge. He could hear the scrabble of squirrels climbing trees, awakened from their winter's sleep, and the lighter rustle of birds flitting among the branches. A cold but not unfriendly breeze pushed his black hair off his shoulders. Bin-daa-dee-nin gazed into the distance, across the broad tan desert, flecked with prickly pear, cholla, and yucca cactus and the stunted mesquite trees. Very far in the distance he could see two widely separated ranch houses, surrounded by outlying buildings. He could not see people, but he knew they were there, and so were their food and goods.

That is where our next meal is coming from, he thought with a grim smile.

He must return to the others. "You're a good horse," he told Moon That Flies, who flicked an ear in response. "Now you must help my brother."

Yuu-his-kishn glared at him when Bin-daa-dee-nin walked into the camp, leading the horse. "Where have you been?" he demanded.

"Working with the horse!" Bin-daa-dee-nin scowled back. After a moment's thought, he pulled off the horse's bridle to leave him free to graze. He noticed that Yuu-his-kishn had fashioned a kind of carrier out of juniper branches laid lengthwise, with cross branches for Nzhų-'a'c-siin to lie on, all tied together with the rope from the miners' wagon. Nzhų-'a'c-siin lay sprawled on the ground, but his eyelids were twitching.

Yuu-his-kishn stalked back and forth. "I do not even want to be here! First Victorio threatens to shoot me and now you wander around so that we will be shot by the soldiers and end up like him!" Yuu-his-kishn pointed furiously at Nzhų-'a'c-siin. "I curse Victorio every day!"

Bin-daa-dee-nin stamped his foot. "Victorio was a great chief!" he shouted. Victorio, a Chiricahua Apache, had swept by the Mescalero reservation two springs ago and persuaded or forced hundreds of warriors to join him on the warpath. Most of the warriors had been eager to go—they were tired of sitting around the reservation with nothing to do, eating spoiled and inadequate food, helpless as their horses and stock were stolen, watching their families and friends die of terrible diseases. But Yuu-his-kishn had been forced to leave the reservation at gunpoint.

"Enough!" Bin-daa-dee-nin snapped. "We are all here now. We can't go back to the reservation!"

"Now we are *bandidos*," Yuu-his-kishn muttered. He propped Nzhų-'a'c-siin up against a boulder and put a biscuit in his hand. "Running with Victorio was a foolish thing to do."

Bin-daa-dee-nin stuck his hand in Yuu-his-kishn's deerskin bag and took several biscuits for himself. Stuffing one in his mouth, he turned to the task of lashing the carrier to the horse, creating a makeshift harness out of long, thin branches and the shirts. *I do not regret those days with Victorio,* he thought defiantly.

Victorio had led his warriors south, across the border of New Mexico with Old Mexico. Under the chief's skillful leadership, they had crossed and recrossed the border, always just ahead of the army, raiding to stay alive. They had lived well, trading on Apache cleverness, skillful riding, and endurance. An Apache could run seventy miles a day through the desert even on foot, easily outpacing the soldiers.

Those had been glorious days of freedom and victory—until Victorio died, shot to death in a battle in Old Mexico, in a place the Mexicans called Tres Castillos. Bin-daa-dee-nin, Yuu-his-kishn, and Nzhų-'a'c-siin had been away on a raid across the border and had missed Victorio's last fight. When the three Apaches had heard that he was dead, they had been unsure what to do. They could try to remain raiders, with a much diminished band, or return to the reservation.

We cannot go back there, Bin-daa-dee-nin reminded himself, tying knots in the heavy cloth. It was strong and should hold during the rough trip ahead. *If we are not hung or imprisoned for leaving, we will starve or fall sick and die anyway.*

Bin-daa-dee-nin kept working on the harness, but his mind filled with memories of reservation days: the Mescalero women in their tattered, dirty calico skirts and blouses, waiting in a long line at the agent's for food that often didn't come and was never enough, unable to forage for mescalero, the spiny cactus that once provided so much food and drink for the tribe; the men squatting on the ground, playing gambling games, forbidden to hunt for their families; the ill, emaciated, crying children confined in the agency sickrooms, kept from the medicine women and men who might have helped them. Despite this bad life, not many of the Mescalero remained free—most of them were now on the reservation, a tiny patch of the Mescaleros' former lands.

I had no reason not to leave with Victorio, Bin-daa-dee-nin thought. *The reservation killed my mother and father.*

Bin-daa-dee-nin glanced at Yuu-his-kishn, who was urging Nzhų-'a'c-siin to eat. While they were on the reservation, Bin-daa-dee-nin remembered seeing Yuu-his-kishn, his tall form wrapped in his holey agency-issued blanket, talking to the Indian agent and soldiers. In that way he had learned to speak English and the ways of the white man. Bin-daa-dee-nin had not known Yuu-his-kishn well then—before the reservation, Yuu-his-kishn's family had hunted on the north side of the mountains and Bin-daa-dee-nin's on the south.

"I'm not hungry," Nzhų-'a'c-siin said, pushing away Yuu-his-kishn's hand with the food.

"You must try to eat," Yuu-his-kishn said. "You have eaten nothing in days."

Nzhų-'a'c-siin took the biscuit and ate a small piece of it. Yuu-his-kishn did not try to force him to eat more, but Bin-daa-dee-nin knew that Nzhų-'a'c-siin's lack of appetite was a worrisome sign.

Bin-daa-dee-nin caught Moon That Flies, who was eating the sparse grass, bridled him again, and fitted the harness around him, tying the back ends to the carrier. The horse blew out a loud snort and looked around at the strange object. "It's all right," Bin-daa-dee-nin reassured him, going to the horse's head for a moment. Moon That Flies pawed the ground with his front foot, but he didn't bolt. Bin-daa-dee-nin and Yuu-his-kishn carried Nzhų-'a'c-siin to the carrier and set him down on it. Then

Bin-daa-dee-nin gathered their supplies, slung the deerskin bags over Moon That Flies' back, and guided him off the ledge. The horse skittered a bit, but then settled down to his work.

Yuu-his-kishn stayed by the carrier, pushing it along and freeing it when it snagged on rocks and trees. Bin-daa-dee-nin looked back. They were going very slowly and leaving a trail even a soldier could see.

"Did you hear that?" Yuu-his-kishn asked suddenly.

Bin-daa-dee-nin stopped the horse. Very faintly in the distance were the sounds of pursuit. Many horses—at least twenty—and the shouts of men. "They're coming," he called back to Yuu-his-kishn. The miners must be with the soldiers. That would account for the shouting—the soldiers had learned by now that making a lot of noise wasn't the way to catch Apaches.

The miners, angry over the death of their brother, would surely want to kill.

"We've got to hide Nzhų-'a'c-siin and run," Bin-daa-dee-nin said, his eyes already searching for another cave. He saw only stumpy, scattered trees and brush.

"They'll find—" Yuu-his-kishn began.

"We have no choice!" Bin-daa-dee-nin said angrily. "Would I leave him if I did?"

"Go, brothers," said Nzhų-'a'c-siin in a surprisingly strong voice. "I do not think the soldiers will find me."

That arroyo over there, Bin-daa-dee-nin thought, pulling the horse and carrier over to a dry, deep ditch. With his hunting knife he slashed the harness free from the carrier. Yuu-his-kishn was already beside him. They laid Nzhų-'a'c-siin in damp sand where the storm water had broken away the bank, leaving an overhang. Bin-daa-dee-nin tossed him one of the rifles and the deerskin bags. "We'll come back for you," he promised, already turning to run.

He and Yuu-his-kishn leapt back onto the bank, and Bin-daa-dee-nin grabbed the horse's reins. He tried not to think about the terrible things the miners would do to Nzhų-'a'c-siin if they found him. The miners valued their worthless lumps of metal so much. The attack on the wagon of silver would surely make them as angry as the death of their brother.

Bin-daa-dee-nin and Yuu-his-kishn raced up a steep hillside with the horse trotting behind. The gray face of a cliff, blank and smooth, blocked their path.

"The horse can't climb that," Yuu-his-kishn said. "Let him go."

"No!" Bin-daa-dee-nin couldn't bear it. The horse was his sign from the gods, his sign that they would succeed in staying free.

"You have to!" shouted Yuu-his-kishn. "We will raid and get other horses."

I must survive, Bin-daa-dee-nin thought, dropping Moon That Flies' reins. But to his astonishment, the horse took a running start and scrambled up the cliff, his strong hindquarters churning as he fought to reach the top.

Bin-daa-dee-nin gave a muffled shout of joy and climbed after him, his hands expertly scrabbling for small crevices in the rock. Yuu-his-kishn climbed quickly beside him. They swung themselves over the top and jumped to their feet. Panting, Bin-daa-dee-nin jerked his head around at the sound of scattering rocks. Someone was scaling the cliff. In a moment the faces and shoulders of three men rose over the top, foolishly exposed. Bin-daa-dee-nin had no trouble identifying them as miners—they wore checked shirts, and their necks still bore traces of grime. One of them had his head bandaged, probably from their confrontation at the wagon. Moon That Flies gave a sharp whinny of alarm and backed away.

Acting as one, Bin-daa-dee-nin and Yuu-his-kishn rushed at

the miners and shoved. With yells, the men tumbled back down the slope. In the distance Bin-daa-dee-nin saw soldiers running to the base of the cliff, their blue uniforms like broken pieces of sky.

"Too many to fight." To his great relief, Bin-daa-dee-nin saw Moon That Flies waiting a short distance off—the horse had not simply run off in a panic. "But we can be far away before the soldiers get up here." *Often the soldiers do not try that hard to catch us,* Bin-daa-dee-nin thought. He hoped this would be one of those times.

Leading Moon That Flies, he ran across the hard gray-brown sand at the top of the cliff. He did not want to ride the horse when they were traveling so fast—he would not have time to guide him around rocks and thorny cactus. But Moon That Flies trotted easily behind, seeming to know the mountain as well as they.

Soon the last clatter of the soldiers' weapons faded, and the sounds of the hunt disappeared. Bin-daa-dee-nin began to circle back toward Nzhų-'a'c-siin. He doubted the soldiers would expect him to return to the same place where the battle had begun. But he did not want to arrive there before dusk.

At last the sun sank behind the long horizon, plunging the huge mountain into purple-red shadow. "Can you see?" whispered Yuu-his-kishn.

"Yes," Bin-daa-dee-nin replied shortly. *What I can see is the night world,* he thought. Moon That Flies' black patches and face had melted into the night, and Bin-daa-dee-nin could see only his white parts. Bin-daa-dee-nin hated creeping around in the woods after dark, but it was often the only way to avoid pursuit.

"Who-*who*!" an owl hooted from a nearby tree. Bin-daa-dee-nin froze, his heart racing. He was afraid to even look for the owl, but he didn't know how to escape it. Owls were the spirits of the unquiet dead returned. *I have known so many who have died violent deaths,* he thought. *Who can it be?* He could feel Moon That Flies' comforting breath on his shoulder. The horse's presence grounded him, and he had the courage to go on.

A bright halo glowed at the eastern horizon over the flat desert. The vast full moon slowly rose, shedding its benevolent light and dispelling the deep black of the shadows. Bin-daa-dee-nin breathed more slowly and concentrated on keeping his direction right down the mountain. He could hear Yuu-his-kishn stumbling behind him—he didn't see as well in the dark. They had almost reached Nzhų-'a'c-siin.

If he is still there. Bin-daa-dee-nin clenched his fists.

Bin-daa-dee-nin gave a low whistle, then handed Moon That Flies' reins to Yuu-his-kishn and slid down the bank to where they had left Nzhų-'a'c-siin. He could see his brother's black eyes glittering in the darkness like an animal's.

"I'm all right," Nzhų-'a'c-siin said. Now that Bin-daa-dee-nin was closer, he could see that Nzhų-'a'c-siin was sitting up, with his back to the dirt wall of the arroyo.

"The soldiers?" Bin-daa-dee-nin asked, crouching beside him.

"Long gone," Nzhų-'a'c-siin assured him.

"Then let's eat." Bin-daa-dee-nin whistled up to Yuu-his-kishn. "This is a good enough place."

Bin-daa-dee-nin quickly built a fire with twigs and branches long-ago rainstorms had washed up near Nzhų-'a'c-siin—that wood was dry. He set one of the deerskin bags of food next to the fire. Yuu-his-kishn reached into his bag and pulled out a small pot and a frypan and filled the pot with enough water and coffee for three cups. Bin-daa-dee-nin laid out strips of bacon from the slab in the frypan. Soon the thick, smoky scent of bacon settled over the camp. Bin-daa-dee-nin stretched out his legs, letting the warm smell of the food fill his nose and mind.

"Many soldiers?" asked Nzhų-'a'c-siin. He seemed much more alert, Bin-daa-dee-nin noticed. That was a very good sign.

"Also miners," Yuu-his-kishn said shortly, flipping the bacon with a small stick. He would not discuss the miners because one was dead—that might attract his vengeful spirit.

Bin-daa-dee-nin watched the horse. He was drinking from a shallow pool of rainwater. The full moon reflected in the pool, small and gleaming, next to the horse's muzzle. Bin-daa-dee-nin wished his brothers would take care of themselves and be quiet like his horse. He could sense an argument coming on.

"So what do you think we should do?" he finally asked Yuu-his-kishn. His brother would have his say—he might as well hear it now.

"I think it is time to go back to the reservation," Yuu-his-kishn said firmly. He handed Nzhų-'a'c-siin a stick draped with three pieces of bacon and placed the rest on a smooth rock. "We could take Nzhų-'a'c-siin to the white doctor there."

"To the white *sickness* there," Bin-daa-dee-nin shot back. He jumped up and paced around the fire. "Have you forgotten? Do you want to cough up blood? Or do you want to die in the reservation prison?"

"What do you want to do?" Yuu-his-kishn asked Nzhų-'a'c-siin.

"I've . . . heard my sister no longer lives," Nzhų-'a'c-siin said with difficulty. "You know there was the trouble at the reservation because of us leaving, and she became ill when the people were put in the corral. Perhaps . . . we should stay out here a little longer."

Bin-daa-dee-nin swung around quickly and looked at him. *I did not hear of this,* he thought. He had learned of the punishment on the reservation for those who stayed and had not followed Victorio. The soldiers had decided that the reservation Indians were giving supplies to Victorio and put them in a corral filled with manure up to their ankles. Many became sick or died.

"I should have brought her with me," Nzhų-'a'c-siin said sadly. "Many women and children did come. I should never have left her."

"This life is worse," Yuu-his-kishn snapped. "My parents and brother are still on the reservation. That's the best place. At least they have a chance of staying alive there. The Indian agents change, and maybe the way they treat us will change. We might not be imprisoned. But out here, we will certainly be cut down by savage white men. Or scouts."

Then go! Bin-daa-dee-nin wanted to shout at him. Anger surged within him. But he could not stay alone with a wounded man. And he knew that Yuu-his-kishn would not leave them, even though he thought they all would die out here. Unless Bin-daa-dee-nin provoked him to a boiling rage.

Yuu-his-kishn was watching Nzhų-'a'c-siin closely. Although Nzhų-'a'c-siin spoke in a strong voice, his face was pale, and his eyelids sometimes closed from pain. Bin-daa-dee-nin did not know if Nzhų-'a'c-siin would even survive the long journey back to the reservation. Yuu-his-kishn was probably thinking the same thing. But if they could remain free for a while longer, without killing Nzhų-'a'c-siin in their flight across the mountain to escape the soldiers, he might recover enough to go back to a life of raiding—or to the reservation. So, in a way, they might agree about what to do.

Moon That Flies snorted as he moved along the arroyo, cropping grass. The horse was gathering his strength for tomorrow, what they all should be doing. Moon That Flies would be vital to their staying alive.

"Tomorrow I ride my horse in the desert," Bin-daa-dee-nin said to the others. "I will see if he is fast as well as brave."

3

The next morning Bin-daa-dee-nin awoke at first light. He sat up quickly, pushing back his hair and retying his red headband so that his hair would stay out of his face. The gray sky, not yet greeting the full sun, shed a dim, unformed look on the black trees and brownish sand. The ashes of the fire twirled in an abrupt, cool breeze, forming a tiny whirlwind that danced down the arroyo. A faint mist rose from the ground, the last of the rain returning to the sky.

Bin-daa-dee-nin turned his head slightly at a soft ripping sound. Moon That Flies was quietly grazing up above the Apaches, out of the arroyo, his black-and-white patches gleaming in the fresh light.

Smiling slightly, Bin-daa-dee-nin listened to what would soon be morning. The wind pushed through the junipers, gnarled and twisted from a long life in this dry land, and the mesquite with its long thorns, bringing the whistle of branches and leaves, not the clank of spurs or calls of men. Yuu-his-kishn and Nzhų-'a'c-siin were still asleep, curled around where the fire had been.

Now I will ride, Bin-daa-dee-nin thought. In a single bound he cleared the edge of the arroyo. Picking up the bridle, his rifle, and his deerskin bag from where he had left them under a mesquite, he walked over to the horse. Moon That Flies' large eyes watched him from under his tangled black forelock. "We must scout," Bin-daa-dee-nin said. Although he and his brothers had the supplies from the miners' wagon, those wouldn't last more than a few days. Also, Bin-daa-dee-nin hoped to find the others horses.

Moon That Flies half reared when Bin-daa-dee-nin stepped on a branch, cracking it, as he approached the horse. Bin-daa-dee-nin tried several times to bridle him, but Moon That Flies nervously tossed his head out of reach. Finally Bin-daa-dee-nin rested his hand on the horse's shoulder, waiting patiently until he stood still. "See? You have nothing to fear," Bin-daa-dee-nin told him. This time he was able to get the bit in Moon That Flies' mouth and the headpiece over his ears. Gripping the horse's long mane, Bin-daa-dee-nin swung easily onto his back. He would have liked a saddle—it would be simpler to carry his rifle—but it wasn't necessary. He tucked the rifle under his arm and squeezed the bag under his leg.

At first Bin-daa-dee-nin sat straight on the horse, his legs tight around his sides in case the animal bucked. But Moon That Flies carefully picked his way down the mountain, avoiding the thorny branches of the mesquite and occasionally hopping over rocks. The mountain still slept in gray and black shadow, although the desert below glowed with pale light. *My horse seems to know the mountain well,* Bin-daa-dee-nin thought. *Perhaps the soldiers rode him here*. He sat back, letting Moon That Flies choose a path.

At the bottom of the mountain Bin-daa-dee-nin looked carefully across the desert, stretching in all directions. The weak light did not allow him to see the dust clouds that would indicate soldiers, but they would not be able to see him, either. The desert was silent, abandoned, the cactus gentle blurs that dotted the sand. Soon the blaze of the sun would reveal the sharp blades of the yucca and spines of the prickly pear in this hard, forbidding place.

Will I ever see home again? Bin-daa-dee-nin wondered. The air was crisp and cold, with a shimmer of ice on the sand. This land wasn't so warm as Mexico, but not as cold as home would be right now, so early in the spring. Bin-daa-dee-nin looked back, but the mountain, rearing into the sky, blocked his view to the north and east. *Home is that way,* he thought. *Sacred White Mountain and tall trees and green valleys.*

The horse snorted and tossed his head, eager to get going. Bin-daa-dee-nin pushed his useless thoughts aside. He lived here now, for this day, and he had much to do. And in this place he had a splendid horse.

The sun tipped over the horizon, spilling yellow across the desert and horizon, as if a hand had flung the color. "Let us go west," Bin-daa-dee-nin said. That was the direction of the two ranches he had seen yesterday. West was yellow in Mescalero rituals. Today he could see and feel the west's yellowness.

Bin-daa-dee-nin loosened the reins and let the horse walk, then trot. Moon That Flies responded eagerly, trying to break into a gallop. Bin-daa-dee-nin held him back for a moment with the reins, then dropped them loose and leaned forward over the horse's neck.

Moon That Flies took off so fast, Bin-daa-dee-nin almost slid off backward over his rump. He grabbed the horse's mane, balancing and steadying himself with his legs. The ground rushed by, a grayish blur of cactus and sand, and Bin-daa-dee-nin laughed from sheer joy. "Perhaps you are a wild horse after all," he called into the wind.

After he had ridden far into the desert, he tried to slow Moon That Flies, then turn him. They were close to a ranch, and the sound of hooves carried a long way. Moon That Flies shook his head, flapping his mane, fighting the restraint. His neck was streaked with sweat, but he seemed barely winded. *Very good,* Bin-daa-dee-nin thought. *When we raid, we will have to run not just here but back as well.* Moon That Flies seemed willing to run forever. At last, with several short jerks on the reins, Bin-daa-dee-nin slowed him. He tried to turn him toward the ranch, but Moon That Flies bent his head and kept going straight. Finally Bin-daa-dee-nin pulled his head around so hard, the horse had no choice but to turn left. Bin-daa-dee-nin's rifle almost slipped out from under his arm.

"Either you have not been ridden before I found you, or it has been a long time," Bin-daa-dee-nin said softly. Tugging firmly on the reins, he brought the horse to a halt.

A burst of breeze flicked Moon That Flies' mane, then Bin-daa-dee-nin's hair. The ball of wind darted across the sand, lifting a fine haze. To the side of it, Bin-daa-dee-nin could see the ranch, motionless in the last silence of night.

He slid off his horse and led him by the reins so that he could control him better. *Good that he is of broken color,* Bin-daa-dee-nin thought. *He'll be harder to see.* Bin-daa-dee-nin walked by several low buildings and approached the corrals. The cattle in the larger corral stirred restlessly and ran to the other side, and Bin-daa-dee-nin moved past them before they could become too excited and draw attention. He had no use for the cattle anyway—they ran too slowly to take along, and he would have no time to butcher one. The next corral held something he had come for.

A horse stood shivering next to the wood boards. He had long legs and a thin neck and didn't look especially quick—he was too awkward—but he might be fast across a stretch. Bin-daa-dee-nin carefully studied the position of the buildings, ranch house, and corral. When he came back, he didn't want to get trapped somehow.

Moon That Flies whinnied loudly and stretched his neck toward the other horse. Bin-daa-dee-nin grabbed his muzzle, praying that the ranchers could not tell one horse's whinny from another's.

Suddenly a light glowed in a window of the house. Bin-daa-dee-nin leapt onto Moon That Flies' back, hoping this abrupt action didn't spook him into a full, thundering gallop that everyone in the ranch house would hear. The horse stayed still, pawing the ground with one hoof. Bin-daa-dee-nin tried to turn him, but Moon That Flies stubbornly shook his head, pulling the reins through Bin-daa-dee-nin's hands. *Perhaps he wants to join that other horse, or perhaps he isn't well trained,* Bin-daa-dee-nin thought. He could smell the ranchers' fire in their house and bread and eggs cooking. The ranchers were awake. The yellow light of the sun grew strong, destroying the shadows with its power—and soon he and his horse would be seen. Bin-daa-dee-nin pounded Moon That Flies with his heels, at the same time hauling his head around as hard as he could. The horse might throw him at such rough treatment, but he had no choice.

Moon That Flies quivered, then jumped into a bouncy trot, moving back out into the desert. Bin-daa-dee-nin urged him to gallop, keeping his hands firm on the reins, careful not to let his horse dart back toward the ranch. Through the window he could see someone moving outside the house. Bin-daa-dee-nin leaned over Moon That Flies' neck so that the rancher wouldn't see that the horse had a rider and to ask him for speed. Finally the horse responded, gathering his legs under him and bounding forward.

Had the running hooves been heard at the house? *Perhaps my ambush is spoiled,* Bin-daa-dee-nin thought. *I could have just taken that horse in the corral now.* But he would not have had much time before the ranchers came outside. Always outnumbered as he was, Bin-daa-dee-nin could not bring himself to raid without scouting first. Besides, when he came back, he wanted to allow enough time to check the buildings for food. Maybe the house too. He did not like to even enter those unclean places, which seemed to him to gather every sickness of their occupants from season to season, but he might find food easily available there.

Bin-daa-dee-nin turned Moon That Flies gradually so that they were circling back toward the ranch. With a series of short jerks, he managed to bring the horse back down into a trot. Two people were now outside the ranch house, a tall and a shorter one, but they were walking about, showing no signs of excitement.

"Good. I was not seen," Bin-daa-dee-nin said to himself. "Come, my horse. We should return to the mountain."

The sun was a yellow glaring eye, rising quickly. A flick of movement near an escarpment caught Bin-daa-dee-nin's eye. Large animals of some kind were coming toward him. *Soldiers!* Bin-daa-dee-nin gripped Moon That Flies' mane, ready to flee. Then he realized that although the animals were in a bunch, they were walking randomly about, grazing. It was a herd of antelope.

The sunlight flashed across the desert. Now he could see the antelopes' brown-and-white coats and long black antlers. The ones with their backs to him flicked their short white tails, and a big one facing toward him pointed its black muzzle up, sniffing the air. The antelopes had not yet scented him.

Bin-daa-dee-nin's heart beat faster. *Food,* he thought. *If I can bring one of those antelope down, we will eat for many days.* Meat was good, nourishing food—not like the scanty berries and roots they could gather on the mountain. *The gods are with me and this horse,* Bin-daa-dee-nin assured himself. The white men had killed so much game, it was hard to find anything bigger than a rabbit to hunt.

The wind darted about, swirling now from the east, then the west. *The antelope will scent us soon,* Bin-daa-dee-nin thought.

And Moon That Flies probably will fight me if I try to walk him closer. We should run at them.

Bin-daa-dee-nin pointed the horse at the herd and let him have his head. In barely a stride Moon That Flies charged from a trot into a full-out gallop and almost shot out from under him again.

Bin-daa-dee-nin's grip on Moon That Flies' mane was all that saved him. He hauled himself back up behind the horse's withers, clamping his arm down on his rifle. *I thought this horse ran fast as we came from the mountain, but now I see what he can do,* Bin-daa-dee-nin thought. Moon That Flies was almost to the antelope.

The big buck in front saw them. In an instant he whirled, bounding high in the air. The rest of the herd leapt after him, their small hooves clattering over the hard soil. Moon That Flies raced forward.

Bin-daa-dee-nin laughed. The horse moved so fast, Bin-daa-dee-nin felt like they were another creature altogether—a spirit of the wind, sun, and sky, free, bright, and unbounded by the earth. He would have liked to let out an Apache yell of victory.

The antelope had scattered and were nearly hidden by dust. But Bin-daa-dee-nin had observed the position of the big buck as he fled. Swinging up his rifle one-handed, Bin-daa-dee-nin fired into the cloud. He heard a heavy thud. *Perfect shot!* he congratulated himself. If the ranchers had heard it, they would just think the soldiers were shooting at something.

Stopping his excited horse was difficult, but at last Bin-daa-dee-nin was able to drop off his back. Both horse and rider eagerly approached the kill.

The buck lay on his side, shot through the heart. He was fat from feeding on the early spring grasses. Bin-daa-dee-nin reached for his large hunting knife, which he had bought from a Mexican trader, and began to cut up the meat. He kept one hand slipped through Moon That Flies' reins to make sure he didn't wander off. But the horse stood quietly, head down, watching what he was doing.

Bin-daa-dee-nin packed as much as he could into his bag, then led Moon That Flies over to a large rock. Standing on the rock, he slung the heavy bag over the horse, then pulled himself onto him, clutching his rifle under his arm. Luckily Moon That Flies tolerated this strange behavior.

"A very good hunt," he told his horse, turning him toward the mountain. It shot up before him out of the desert like a jagged, frozen gray waterfall, silent, huge, and menacing. It was hard to go back there after the bright freedom of the desert. But his brothers were there, and tonight they would make a fire to cook the meat. They would have a feast—if they were not on the run. The soldiers might give them a rest for a while, after their defeat last night, while they regrouped and rearmed. But they never gave up.

Part II

THE DIARY OF SARAH CHILTON

4

Sarah Chilton sat upright in bed, listening. The darkness around her was unbending, opaque. "What was that?" she whispered.

A noise had awoken her, coming from the hard-packed sandy yard around the ranch house. Or had it been a dream? The desert outside, stretching from her family's ranch in the Bootheel of New Mexico, was full of dreams.

Tucking her soft cotton quilt around her waist, Sarah peered across the room at Rachel, her six-year-old sister. She could barely see Rachel's form in her bed against the wall, but Sarah could hear gentle breathing from a pile of quilts and pillows.

Sarah smiled to herself. Her sister slept more soundly than anyone Sarah knew. Rachel had easily napped first in the swaying, smoky train, then in the jolting, creaking Conestoga wagon that had brought the Chilton family seven hundred miles from their home in Fort Smith, Arkansas, last November to join Sarah's father, who had prepared the ranch house in New Mexico for them.

Suddenly a glare of moonlight funneled straight through the tiny window above Sarah's bed. The window was made of real glass and set in the two-foot-thick adobe wall. Sarah loved the way it let cheerful yellow afternoon light into the plain room, but she hadn't realized the moonlight sometimes came through it too. She blinked, trying to adjust to the brightness, then realized she now had enough light to see clearly.

I'll write in my diary, she thought, reaching under her feather tick for the slim, leather-bound black book. Setting it on her quilt, she leaned out of bed and groped along the wall under the window until she found her inkwell and pen on the floor. The stage had brought her fresh writing supplies just last week. Then she settled back in bed to write, rearranging her quilt over her legs and propping her pillow against the wood headboard. Her long blond hair slipped over her shoulders as she bent over her book.

February 13, 1881

Dear Diary,
I have not written in you for several days because we have been so busy on the ranch with the spring roundup. My job was to help my father and our good neighbors the Stautons hold the yearling calves still for branding. I can only imagine what my dear friend Lucy would think of this. Our lives in Fort Smith were very civilized!

Sarah nibbled the feather quill of her pen, frowning. Even after three months on the ranch, she still missed her friends and relatives in Fort Smith more than she could say. Sarah's father had given up a lucrative medical practice when he had moved first himself, last summer, and then his family to the New Mexico Territory to try ranching.

Mama's health does not seem much improved by our move to the country, Sarah wrote.

I know that is an important reason we came here. Perhaps now that it is spring, Mama will grow strong. I know I am enjoying this time: five of the cows have already given birth to adorable little calves that wobble and moo after their mothers. Speaking of birthdays, tomorrow I shall be fourteen. I wonder what kind of ranch birthday my family has planned for me? Perhaps something good will arrive on the stage.

Sarah remembered her thirteenth birthday last year in Fort Smith. Sarah's mother had been too sick to come downstairs for the party, but two of Sarah's aunts had helped her host a party for six of Sarah's friends and their families in the Chiltons' spacious, white colonial house, set on a large, deep green lawn of Kentucky bluegrass. A string quartet had played while the guests chatted and then assembled for a sit-down dinner at the long oak table in the dining room, set with her mother's beautiful wheat-pattern china. Sarah, wearing a sky blue silk dress and matching slippers, had felt so grown up as she had sat to her father's right at the head of the table.

After dinner she had gone for a horseback ride in the nearby park with her best friend, Lucy Starr, on two of Mr. Chilton's fine saddle horses. Trotting sidesaddle along the groomed dirt paths in the park, in the cool, dark shade of hundred-year-old oaks, Sarah longed for a horse of her own, one that would truly respond to her every wish and command. She had been an equestrian most of her life, but her father had always seemed reluctant to let her have a horse. He'd said that she was too young to know what she really wanted and that at her age she'd just outgrow a pony. Besides, he would point out, she could always borrow one of his saddle horses whenever she wanted to ride.

Papa never seemed to understand that a borrowed horse wasn't the same as having your very own. Sarah hoped for a horse surpassing any of those in her father's stable—those horses walked, trotted, and cantered obediently but didn't have much personality. When she was little, she'd wanted to find a magical one like Pegasus, the winged horse, to fly her through the heavens to the home of the Greek gods.

Sarah smiled to herself. Maybe that was a childish fancy. But that was how she still felt.

Her father had promised her a horse once the family was settled on the ranch. Sarah knew that he wanted to give her a reason to like the ranch instead of missing Fort Smith, and when she had arrived here in New Mexico, she had looked forward to choosing her own riding horse. But Sarah had been disappointed when she found that all the horses at the ranch were scrubby, tough little mustangs with backbreaking gaits. The ranch hands might sing those horses' praises because they could go all day without tiring, but Sarah didn't care much for them as pleasure mounts.

When she asked if a horse could be sent from Fort Smith, her father said that a fine saddle horse from there would drop dead in the heat or colic on the sandy grass the horses here had to forage. He also reminded her that he was out of money after buying the ranch, livestock, and supplies and couldn't afford the cost of bringing a horse all that way. The only horse the Chiltons owned now was a leggy, thin half Thoroughbred to pull the buckboard, and Sarah had to admit, a horse of that breed didn't seem to be adjusting to ranch life too well.

Sarah's head jerked up, and she almost dropped her inky pen. There was the noise again! Now she was sure she had heard it. This time it sounded like an animal with four hooves, quietly clopping across the yard. Maybe one of the cattle or the horse was loose?

Sarah set her diary and inkwell carefully on the window ledge, threw back her quilt and tiptoed through the open doorway of her bedroom into the tiny, dark living room. This room's window was on the side of the house away from the moon.

Should I wake up Father? Sarah wondered as she crossed the board floor, accidentally tipping her mother's rocking chair. She stopped to steady it, then stood before the heavy wood front door, hesitating.

If any of the stock were out, her father would surely want to know about it. He had enough problems losing cattle and horses to accidents, disease, and straying. But her father had been up all today and long into the night, helping with the branding. Sarah knew that he was exhausted. The sound outside seemed to come from just one animal. *I can easily catch it and put it back in the corral myself,* she thought.

On the other hand, she was forbidden to go out at night. Sarah knew that her family's ranchland was part of Apachería, the home of the Apache Indians. For years they had roamed the mountains and canyons, the scrub desert and intermittent rivers, ranging from Texas to Arizona and down into Old Mexico, just forty miles from the ranch's border. Sarah had heard plenty of horror stories about the Apaches from the Chiltons' neighbors and the stagecoach drivers. The canyon to the east of the ranch on the stagecoach route near Cooke's Peak was said to be littered with the bodies of travelers ambushed by the Apaches. Most of those bodies had turned to bones, the moisture dried out of them by the hot, dry desert air. They lay by the trail, unburied and unclaimed—often no one knew who they had been.

At the stage stop ten miles from the ranch, the owners had built a huge corral surrounded by eight-foot-high adobe walls with a large gate. The stage could race into the corral if chased by Apaches, in deadly pursuit with rifles and bows and arrows. The Apaches were also said to rob the mule caravans coming south from the copper mine at Santa Rita and the silver and lead mines at Cooke's Peak.

But Sarah had never seen a single Indian—not on the ranch, not at the stage stop, and not even on the entire journey from Fort Smith. She was beginning to think the neighbors had made up those stories about the Apaches just to frighten their children into minding. Or maybe the Indians had really been a threat in the past, but now they were gone. After all, the Silver City newspaper, printed in the small town about twenty miles northwest of the ranch, had reported last fall the death of Victorio, a Chiricahua Apache chief. Victorio had been killed in a battle with the Mexican army right before Sarah and her mother and sister had moved out to the ranch. Geronimo, another Chiricahua chief, had been confined to the San Carlos reservation in Arizona for years.

I could just go back to bed and worry about the stray animal in the morning, Sarah thought. *But I can't sleep anyway—the moon's too bright.* Besides, she wanted to be responsible and help her father, as she had tried to do since her arrival at the ranch. He had so much to do with Mama sick. Sarah's mother hadn't been well for almost as long as Sarah could remember—Mama had lost the first baby when Sarah was only nine.

Sarah nodded firmly now that she'd made her decision. Pulling open the front door, she winced as it creaked loudly on its iron hinges. A blast of cool air rushed into the room, stirring the ashes in the fireplace and rustling a pile of letters on the kitchen table. She glanced at her parents' silent bedroom, the only other room in the house save the kitchen, and waited, holding the door open, until she was satisfied that they were still asleep. *I'll retrieve the animal and be back in bed before anyone misses me,* she assured herself.

Outside, the full moon was even more brilliant against the backdrop of the enormous, clear black sky, peppered with glowing stars. Sarah could even see her shadow, grotesquely long, wavering before her. The cattle and horse were shuffling a bit in the corrals to her right, but Sarah could tell that nothing had really alarmed them. Beyond the big corral the desert began, wide open, the tall, bladed yucca cactuses scattered at random, sentinels at their posts to infinity.

Such a strange land, Sarah thought, rubbing her arms. *I wonder if it will ever feel like home.*

The night air still had the glassy, hard edge of winter, and Sarah clutched her long white nightgown closely around her body as she walked across the yard. She had seldom been out at night on the ranch. The sandy, slightly damp earth smelled rich and sweet, as if the new life in the ground was just beginning to seep upward out of its winter cavern. Sarah smiled, letting herself drift through the lingering scents and sensations.

But where was the animal?

Down by the Mimbres River, a hundred yards to her left, clumps of willow and cottonwood wavered gently in the wind. The river had some water in it from winter storms, but Sarah knew she could wade across it. The ranch's proximity to the river in this dry land made life here possible.

"Well, that's where I would hide if I were sneaking in the night," Sarah whispered, looking doubtfully at the trees. Would Indians be by the river? She tried to remember the stories she had heard. No, they'd be trying to steal the stock. That didn't seem to be happening, so she might as well look for the animal in the trees. Sarah walked to the edge of the moonlit yard and hesitated. Then she stepped forward into utter blackness. She drew in a quick breath as cold, thick mud sucked at her ankles. But now she could see a little as her eyes adjusted. The river was thickly surrounded by brush and low trees, and a few cottonwoods towered over her, reaching for the moon with clawed branches that had not yet leafed out.

Then a stand of young willows right next to Sarah began to shake. Sarah leapt back, stifling a scream.

The thing in the trees seemed to start and draw back as well. *I might seem as a ghost to it also,* Sarah thought wryly, despite her fear. She forced herself to think rationally. An Apache would have made her a prisoner already or cut her throat, if the tales she'd heard could be believed. Since the Chiltons' stock was relatively quiet, she must be dealing with a stray from a neighboring ranch.

But Sarah couldn't shake an irrational feeling of dread. Or was it awe? Gripping her hands tightly together, she quickly recited a verse from the prophet Isaiah: *Keep silence before me, O islands; and let the people renew their strength: let them come near; then let them speak: let us come near together to judgment.* The strong words of Isaiah would protect her, she assured herself, trying to stop her knees from quaking.

The willows shook harder and parted as a creature moved through them. Sarah gasped. What appeared to be a large map was moving jerkily between the trees, right toward her. Patches of white floated in the air, propelled by a mysterious dark conveyance. Sarah wondered what kind of apparition her words had called forth. She was too far from the house to scream for help, but her legs felt too weak and wobbly to carry her away.

Just when she thought she would die of fear, the creature poked its head at her and snorted. Startled, Sarah fell backward and sat down hard in the icy mud. "A horse?" she whispered.

As if her words made it all right, the horse stepped completely out of the trees and sniffed her ankle. Now Sarah could see that what she'd thought was a map were really just big areas of white on an otherwise black horse. He was a pinto, with a black mane, tail, and face. A single star of white gleamed on his forehead. The horse's four white legs skittered as Sarah struggled to get up, her wet nightgown pulling her back into the mud.

"Easy, boy," she reassured the horse. "I just have—to get out of—this mud!" Sarah shoved hard with her hands against the ground and managed to stand. She yanked her last foot free from the sticky stuff and stepped up to the horse.

He quickly dropped his muzzle to the top of her head, sniffing, then carefully moved on to her shoulder. They both let out a big sigh of relief at the same time. "Not too frightening, really," Sarah said.

She studied the horse. Even by moonlight, she could see that he was a quality animal. His legs were long, straight, and clean, his back high and straight. He had a finely shaped head with a broad forehead and a tapering, slender muzzle. The horse's large black eyes, reflecting ripples of moonlight, looked back at her, bright with intelligence, spirit, and a trace of lingering suspicion. The color of his coat was truly striking, Sarah thought. He was mostly white on top and dark on the underside, but he had a jagged yet unmistakable black saddle pattern on his back right where a saddle would go.

"Where did you come from?" Sarah murmured, lifting her hand so that the horse could sniff it and become acquainted. She knew she would remember a horse like this if she had seen it before. The Chiltons' neighbors the Gunthers, who lived fifteen miles away, had a pinto, but it was a mule. Sarah couldn't think of a single other pinto animal in the area.

Was the horse a stray, from a long ways off? If so, he must have come very far, across miles of waterless desert or perhaps from the Mimbres Mountains or Cooke's Peak to the east. But horses didn't live in the mountains, home to such wild animals as mountain lions and bear.

"Well, somehow you really must be a stray," Sarah told him.

Didn't that mean she could keep him?

The horse shifted restlessly and stepped to her left. Sarah put aside her thoughts, realizing that she'd better secure the horse before he continued on his rambles. "I've no rope," she said in exasperation, smacking the heel of her hand against her forehead. The horse shied back, and Sarah reached a soothing hand to his shoulder. His coat was winter long and rough to her fingers. The horse craned his neck around to examine her hand.

"I come to catch a beast with no rope. I'm not much of a ranch girl, am I?" Sarah asked, looking around for something she could use to lead the horse.

A quick, chilly breeze shook the clump of willows, rattling their slender, drooping branches. "One of those might do to hold you," Sarah told the horse, reaching for the closest branch. She shivered as her wet, muddy nightgown swung around her legs. *If Mama and Papa hear about this escapade, I'll be in so much trouble,* Sarah thought, trying to break the branch from the tree. It proved pliable and fibrous, and she had difficulty freeing it, but finally she managed to rip off a five-foot length. For a moment she hesitated, wondering how to catch a horse in this way, but when she looped the branch around the horse's neck, he stood quietly.

The moon was high now, directly overhead, its light a cold, clear radiance in the black sky. A few blue-and-white stars twinkled fiercely around it, undaunted by the moon's glare. The shush of the willows, the rattle of a few of last winter's leaves on the giant cottonwoods by the river, and the restless steps of the horse's hooves, sucking in the mud, were the only sounds. Sarah tipped back her head and looked at the moon. Its bright eye seemed to find her, looking back until she felt she shared in its clarity, starkness, and strength.

"I think it must be my birthday now," she whispered. "Are you my birthday present from the ranch, pinto horse?"

The horse tossed his head restively, pulling away against the makeshift rope. Sarah tightened her grip. "I'd best get you settled," she said. "I just have to hope that in the morning, Papa agrees you're my birthday present." She didn't see why not. The ranch had plenty of grass for a horse to eat, and this one would be used to it. And he hadn't cost a cent.

Sarah pulled gently on the willow branch. "Come, dancer in the moon," she said. "Moon horse—Moon Dancer!" The horse jumped forward, landing lightly on his feet. Dancing and fussing, he skittered at the end of the rope but followed Sarah up the hill toward the ranch house. Sarah walked backward to keep an eye on him.

"I can't put you in the corral with the other horse right away—you're too fine to injure in a fight." Sarah frowned, trying to think of other possibilities. She definitely couldn't leave him tied outside, prey for any mountain lion or Apache. Sarah's eye fell on the chicken house. "That will do," she said. "If I can get you to go in it."

The horse snorted.

Sarah led him up to the chicken house and slowly opened the sagging board door, trying not to stir the sleeping chickens into a frenzy. She could barely see them, white and dark balls of feathers, roosting close to one another on a shelf at the back. In front was an empty space where her father sometimes stored the horse's harness and spare wagon parts, but he'd recently emptied it out to make room for more chickens. Sarah thought she could just squeeze in the horse.

Now to see if he'll go, she thought doubtfully. Putting a horse inside a chicken house was very outside her experience with horses. Besides, what he would do depended on his training—and she had no idea what that was.

Sarah stepped inside the small, dark room. She suddenly realized that it would be a tight fit with the horse in there with her—she'd just have to hope he was gentle and didn't rear up and strike her with his front hooves or start kicking. A soft whoosh of wings blew Sarah's hair as one of the chickens flew by her head and landed somewhere behind her. Sarah prayed the chickens would stay put when she brought in the horse.

I must be insane to try this, she realized. But her options were limited. "Come on, boy," she coaxed the horse, pulling gently on the willow branch. "In here."

To her surprise, he responded readily to her tug and stepped into the chicken house. Sarah pushed him over closer to the roost and stumbled to the door, ready to run out if the chickens, and then the horse, exploded into action. A few of the chickens clucked and fluffed their wings, but they didn't seem to mind her experiment.

"How odd," Sarah murmured. The chickens usually threw a noisy fit at the slightest provocation. But maybe they were tired out this time of night—Sarah knew she was. She stifled a huge yawn, wondering how long had she been out here. "Sleep well," she told the horse. "I'll get you a nice breakfast in the morning."

The horse bobbed his black head and nickered.

I must make a point of being the first person awake tomorrow morning, Sarah reminded herself as she latched the chicken house door. Then she could remove the horse from the chicken house and tie him somewhere respectable so that his first introduction to her family would be a good one.

The ranch was still and desolate under the moon, and suddenly Sarah was gripped with fear. She ran back to the house, her bare feet grinding the rough sand, afraid to look behind her. Once inside she latched the door fast, locking out the terrors of the night. Then she tiptoed through the dim living room back to her bedroom, her head full of the night's wonders and experiences.

Rachel was still sleeping soundly in her bed, her small

fingers curled around the edge of a quilt. Careful not to wake her, Sarah reached for her diary and pen on the window ledge.

The moon's last beam shone through the window as the moon continued its journey over the top of the house. Sitting on the cold board floor, Sarah positioned her diary so that she could see to write. She felt a broad smile on her face even though she was tired, filthy, and probably in huge trouble with her father. *What an adventure!* she thought. She had never had such times in Fort Smith. She tried to steady her hand as she picked up her pen, but her hand was still shaking from cold and excitement and her first attempt at writing left a big blotch.

Dear Diary,
Tonight I have found a horse. "Found" is perhaps not the right word. I cannot help but feel that he was sent to me, whether by God or this new land. The moon's magic was upon me tonight, if that is not a heathenish thing to say. But because the moon was full, I was able to find my way to the horse down by the river. I would like to keep him and make him my own riding horse. He does seem trained in some respects. I wonder if he is trained to ride?

A draft swept in from the living room, and Sarah shuddered. She was still in her wet nightgown and cold to the bone. She set down her diary and pen and quickly crossed the room to her simple square pine chest, where she kept her clothes. Opening it, she removed a clean, folded yellow nightgown.

In the wavy mirror over the chest she glimpsed her reflection. Her face was that of a stranger, with long blond hair sticking out around her head in wild, staticky strands and dabs of mud smeared on her forehead and chin. Her gray eyes laughed back at her.

Sarah shook her head. *Quite a spectacle,* she thought. She changed out of her heavy, bedraggled nightgown and dropped it behind her chest. Tomorrow, when no one was looking, she'd retrieve it and wash it.

She got in bed and pulled the quilt up to her waist, then reached for her writing materials and carefully set her inkwell by her pillow. She opened her diary across her knees and bent forward to write.

If the horse is not trained, then I shall do it myself. Papa won't have time. I only hope my beautiful horse is not too wild for the sidesaddle. But he seems well mannered. I am not afraid—I think perhaps he is just the best birthday present ever. On this my birthday I vow: I will make that horse mine in every way, caring for him, riding him, and above all, loving him.

Too weary to get out of bed again, Sarah set her inkwell on the floor, balancing her pen on top of it. She pushed her diary under her feather tick, wrapped her quilt tight around her chin, and closed her eyes. Her soft, warm bed had never felt so delicious.

You'd best wake up in time not only to move the horse, but to think of a good tale to tell Mama and Papa about how you found him, she told herself, feeling sleep close around her like warm, invisible hands. *I must invent a story much different from the real one,* she added, yawning. Tomorrow promised to dawn a most exciting day.

5

Sarah woke up with a start and half climbed out of bed, tangling her feet in her quilt. *Boom, boom, boom, craaack!* What was that awful noise?

In a flash she remembered: the horse, the moon, the chicken house. *I overslept, and now the horse is pitching a fit!* she realized. *I've got to get out there before he destroys the building.*

Her bedroom was full of light, and she could smell the thick, smoky scent of bacon and biscuits cooking in the kitchen. She had no doubt now that it was morning and not first thing, either. Sarah pulled the quilt off her feet and dropped it on the bed, then rushed over to her chest to get out something to wear.

On top of the stack of clothes was a long cotton dress with a blue skirt and blue-and-white-striped bodice. Sarah yanked her nightgown over her head and quickly began dressing. *Thankfully, I don't have to bother with a corset or pantaloons, as I would in Fort Smith!* she thought. Lacing her low black boots took a little more time. Outside, she could hear more banging, a muffled shout, and an angry scream. Rachel?

Sarah tore through the living room, tripping over the braided rug. Grabbing hold of the door frame, she regained her balance and ran out into the yard. The sun was already high and strong, a brilliant, incandescent yellow ball in a whitened sky. Its clear, hot light glittered off millions of quartz crystals in the sand, causing a glare so intense, for a few seconds Sarah held up a hand to shield her eyes, wincing. Her father and sister were standing in front of the chicken house, and the small shed was a sight to behold. The boards at the front of the chicken house were actually *moving* in and out, from each blow of the horse's hooves, Sarah felt sure.

Sarah's stomach churned. This was *not* how she'd wanted her father to meet the horse. He looked positively furious as he reached for the chicken house door, as if he expected some kind of dangerous animal to be inside. A couple of the ranch hands hired to help with the cattle branding, colorful in their plaid shirts and tan-, butternut-, and sable-colored riding chaps, stood around Sarah's father, not working or helping, just tipping back their straw cowboy hats and watching the action from under the brims.

Gathering up her long skirt in one hand, Sarah ran to the chicken house just as Papa yanked open the door. "Don't!" she called, but too late.

The pinto horse raced out of the door in a burst of feathers, dust, and flying hooves. Bucking and plunging, he circled the yard, his patched coat blending into a grayish black blur of motion.

"Whoo-*ee*!" shouted Fred, a whiskery old miner who'd signed on at the ranch last week after suffering a bad case of poisoning from the lead used to leach silver in the Silver City mines. All the ranch hands jumped back as the pinto flashed by them.

They could do something besides flee, Sarah thought, clenching her jaw. But she knew the cowboys had a policy about not getting killed foolishly. Rachel screamed again, and Moon Dancer reared up, his front hooves lashing the turquoise sky.

He is my *horse—I can't let him get away again,* Sarah told herself. *If no one else will do anything, then I must solve this*. Trying to mind a couple of chickens that were underfoot—that was probably why Rachel was screaming—Sarah stepped determinedly nearer the horse. At least he had dropped back to all four feet, but his eyes were wild, the whites of them showing crazily, and he seemed about to take off again. Sarah had not the least idea what to do to calm a savage animal, so she merely lifted her hand and set it on his shoulder in an attempt to pet him into calmness.

Moon Dancer stopped fighting abruptly. He stood blowing, his nostrils red, his sides heaving in and out, and looked at her as if for instructions. "Give me a rope," Sarah said to nobody in particular, not taking her eyes off the horse.

"Little lady's got a way with a bronc," commented Hank, a short, young, bowlegged cowboy, who had worked at several neighboring ranches on branding this spring. His long-roweled spurs clanking, he walked up and put a braided rawhide rope into Sarah's outstretched hand.

Sarah herself could hardly believe that the horse had calmed down so fast, but she wasn't about to admit it. She eased the rope around his neck, and Moon Dancer tolerated it, as he had last night. Sarah let out a breath of relief.

"Sarah, what in Sam hill was a horse doing in the chicken house?" Papa demanded, putting his hands on his hips and glaring at her. Her father, his face tanned and forehead furrowed from the scorching sun and dry winds of the West, hardly looked like the scholarly, pale Fort Smith doctor Sarah had known before his move out to New Mexico eight months ago. As always, Papa wore a plaid long-sleeve work shirt, blue jeans and tan leather chaps, and a straw cowboy hat instead of the vest with a pocketwatch, starched white shirt, and dark wool pants he'd worn in Fort Smith. He could have been one of the cowboys.

"I found him," Sarah said, still breathing hard. This was the tricky part about the horse, and she was unprepared with her story.

She realized she hadn't exactly answered her father's question.

"Found him where?" Papa asked. "Surely he didn't fall out of the sky."

Almost, Sarah thought. "He was wandering around the property," she said vaguely, rubbing her free hand on her skirt. "He was down by the river. I heard him whinny, so I went out and got him."

Papa frowned. "Whose is he?"

"Nobody's, I think," she said. "Just a stray."

"Hmm." Papa carefully examined the horse. "I don't recognize him," he said finally. "He has good feet, though. They're trimmed to perfection. Either somebody's taken decent care of him, or he's been on the run for a while."

Sarah looked at Moon Dancer too. In the stark desert sunlight, a pure yellow bar from heaven to the sand underfoot, he was more beautiful than ever. The black parts of his coat gleamed like midnight, and his white patches sparkled like gypsum sand. He waited patiently, his eyes calm, as if he had nothing to do with that bad horse of a few minutes before.

Rachel had picked up a copper-colored hen and the red-speckled rooster and settled each in the crook of her arm. She was murmuring soothing words, and the chickens were clucking softly back. Sarah was relieved that the chickens seemed all right. They were Rachel's special passion and task, and Sarah knew her sister would never forgive her if they'd been harmed. Rachel's face, red as a ripe strawberry from the heat and her fright, made her buttermilk blond eyebrows, eyelashes, and curly hair a study in contrasts. She was still upset. Sarah bit her lip, realizing that her actions had been irresponsible.

"What do you propose doing with that animal?" Papa asked. He didn't seem angry, Sarah was relieved to note, just genuinely curious. "He's as wild as they come."

"He is not." Sarah kept her hand on Moon Dancer's shoulder, close to his mane. That seemed to be his signal to calm down, and she wasn't taking any chances.

As if to prove her words, a snow-white hen hopped on Moon Dancer's back with a cluck and flutter of wings and settled herself comfortably. Moon Dancer flicked back an ear, but he remained quiet.

"Feisty girl you got there, Will," commented Ned, another one of the hands, stroking his curling gray mustache. "She'd be a help throwing the calves down for branding, I believe."

Sarah heard Hank stifle a laugh and scowled. *Their silly words will not help my case with Father,* she thought.

"Please get to work, everyone," Mr. Chilton said firmly. "I'll join you shortly."

The cowboys moved off slowly toward the big corral, puffs of dust rising from their boots. Mr. Chilton looked at Sarah again, his dark eyes stern. "Well?" he asked. "What do you plan to do with this animal?"

"He's not behaving badly for the fright he's had," Sarah pointed out. "Rachel, you ought not to scream like a crazy person," she added.

Rachel glared at her, pushing her curls out of her face. The stiff breeze, blowing hard across the vast, flat sea of the desert, flipped her hair right back. "I thought he was hurting my chickens," she said. Then she shrugged and pointed at the roosting chicken on Moon Dancer's back. "But I guess he likes them."

"He must have lived with chickens somewhere," Sarah suggested quickly. "I bet he's from a ranch a long ways from here." *So he's a ranch horse, not a wild beast, and I should keep him,* she added to herself. Sarah could hardly believe her luck, but Papa didn't seem to be about to quiz her on exactly when the horse got in the chicken house. Out of the corner of her eye Sarah saw Mama slowly walking toward them across the yard. Even in her faded calico dress and red sunbonnet, Mama was beautiful, but she seemed so frail, not robust like the neighboring ranch women. She was well along with child, and her face and hands were thin and pale.

"Elizabeth, you ought not to be out in the heat of the day," Papa said, the lines in his forehead deepening.

"I'm not overdoing," Mama assured him, tightening the strings of her bonnet under her chin. Ringlets of her chestnut hair poked out around the frilly edges. "I was just making breakfast for the girls, until I heard the unholy ruckus out here. What's this about, birthday girl?" she asked Sarah, smiling. "That's a beautiful horse."

Sarah swallowed guiltily. She was thankful that Mama didn't go too close to him. Sarah tightened her grip on the rope, hoping the horse wasn't out of patience. But Moon Dancer regarded her with a gentle brown eye, as if he had all the time in the world to socialize. "Mama, please go inside and rest yourself," Sarah pleaded. "I didn't mean to cause such a commotion. I just found the horse loose, that's all."

"What's his name?" Mama asked, looking over the pinto. "He has such striking markings."

"Moon Dancer," Sarah replied, then realized she'd just given away when she'd found the horse. But no one seemed to notice.

"A fine name," Mama said approvingly.

"Put that pinto in the little corral for now—I turned the other horse out to graze. I've got to work," Papa said. In the center of the big corral, Sarah could see that the ranch hands had tied down one of the calves and were heating the branding iron in a fire. Suddenly Papa smiled, his teeth white in his suntanned face. "Happy birthday, big girl," he said.

Sarah grinned back. She could keep the horse!

"Happy birthday to you," Rachel caroled, spinning in a circle, her blond curls flying out around her head. Sarah laughed. Her sister was as sweet as a spring flower.

"I guess the excitement's over. You girls come up to the house for some breakfast now—a special birthday breakfast." Mama leaned over and kissed the top of Sarah's head, then started slowly for the house and shade, to Sarah's relief. Rachel skipped after her. "Sarah, put on your bonnet," Mama called over her shoulder. "You're going to be as red and freckled as that bantam rooster."

Mr. Chilton's eyes followed his wife, then he turned to Sarah. "One more question," he said, his voice stern again.

"Yes?" Sarah said meekly, frantically trying to assemble her thoughts. She couldn't make sense of their jumble. She did know exactly what Papa was going to ask.

"I'd like to know when the horse got in the chicken house," Papa said, looking her straight in the eye. "It just occurred to me that he wasn't there when we finished chores last night. And you awoke hours after I did this morning. I was up at first light. And I guess I'm wondering why you named him Moon Dancer."

"Well . . . I . . . put him there by the light of the moon," Sarah answered slowly, dreading Papa's response. Moon Dancer shuffled a bit and tossed his head, as if he sensed they might be in trouble.

"You did what?" Mr. Chilton was staring at her in horror.

"It was so bright outside, and I heard him calling. I thought I'd secure him until morning in the chicken house so he wouldn't run off again," Sarah continued bravely. At least he already knew about that part.

"Child, *Apaches* are around," Mr. Chilton said. Sarah could see that he was trying to be patient, but there was no mistaking the fear in his eyes.

"I didn't see anybody," Sarah assured him. "I looked all around me. I was very careful."

Mr. Chilton kicked his cowboy boot in the dirt and ran a hand through his untidy black hair. "Daughter," he said at last, "you have been living in the West a very short time. You do not know how things are here. This is not Fort Smith."

"I *do* know that, Papa," Sarah said firmly. "I wouldn't have found a stray horse by the Arkansas River—at least not a beautiful pinto like this." She patted the pinto's satiny black-and-white shoulder, and he nudged her gratefully.

"That is not my meaning." Mr. Chilton put his hand under her chin so that she had to look him in the eye. "The Indian threat is real. When they attack, you will not know they are coming. They are absolutely silent, skillful, and deadly. They have no mercy and will kill you in a second if they find you alone outside."

"They haven't done any killing since I've been here," Sarah said defiantly.

"We do not get a newspaper every day, and so we are not always aware of what is happening even over the next mesa," Mr. Chilton replied. "The Apaches have been quiet for a while, probably because Geronimo is back on the San Carlos reservation and Victorio is dead."

Sarah rocked from the toes of her boots to the heels. If those two chiefs were on the reservation or dead, she didn't see why she had to worry about Indians on the warpath.

"Although the main tribes of Apaches are on the reservations now, rogue bands still roam the mountains. There's no telling when they'll strike again. Do you understand me?"

"Yes, Papa," Sarah said obediently.

"What's done is done, I guess," Papa said under his breath. "But I do not want to hear of you going outside at night again."

"Of course not, Papa," Sarah assured him. She didn't want to worry him like this again, but now that she had the horse, she couldn't see any reason why she'd need to be out at night anyway.

"When we're done with branding, I'll have one of the hands get on him and see if he's broke," Papa said.

But that won't be for days, Sarah thought. The cowboys still had dozens of calves to brand. She wanted to ride Moon Dancer right away.

"I'm not sure that horse is suitable for a young lady," Papa went on. The hen on Moon Dancer's back fluttered softly to the ground.

"Oh, but he is. I know he's broke to ride," Sarah said quickly. "Just look at him." Moon Dancer was still standing quietly, although he had begun to lightly paw the ground with one front hoof.

"We'll see. He looks like an Indian pony." Mr. Chilton studied the horse again. "They're partial to colorful animals."

"He behaves like a ranch animal," Sarah said. Suddenly she wasn't sure if Papa was sold on the horse or not. Was Moon Dancer really her birthday present? "Didn't you see how fast he calmed down?" she asked.

Her father shrugged. "He's got to ride like a ranch horse. But we can talk of this more later."

Papa walked over to join the cowboys at the branding, and Sarah led Moon Dancer to the small corral, keeping the rope tight around his neck. The pinto frisked along behind her, playfully grabbing the rope in his teeth, but Sarah had no trouble holding him. She took down the three boards that made up the corral gate, guided Moon Dancer through, and replaced the boards once he was inside, rattling them to make sure they would hold. "I owe you a good breakfast," she told him. "Then I think I'll get out my sidesaddle and try you right away." After all, Papa hadn't told her she couldn't. *If I can't handle the horse, I'll just get off,* Sarah said to herself as she walked to the barn to fetch some hay.

The barn was a small, low affair, a simple rectangle built of ponderosa pine boards to protect from the sandy winds and burning sun the few bales of alfalfa hay and the little silo of corn Papa had harvested from a field near the river. This barn looked nothing like the tall, grand, red-painted structures Sarah was used to in Fort Smith. *Well, we don't have need of a big barn here,* Sarah thought as she lifted the iron latch on the wood door. In Fort Smith there was no open range, and so the animals had to be fed hay and grain in the winter. Here the horses and cattle were let out to fend for themselves all year round, but they could roam for miles, seeking out the clumps of tough sacaton grass. Papa only kept a bit of hay and corn to feed up an ailing animal.

Sarah stepped carefully over the toothed iron plow, which Papa used on the few tillable acres by the river. He stored most of the ranch implements in here: the heavy leather harness for the wagon horse; bridles, neatly hung from nails on the wall; spare fence posts for the corrals; and a hoe for the vegetable garden. Soon Mama and Rachel would be planting the garden on the easterly, shadiest side of the house: rows of squash, lettuce, cucumbers, and all manner of vegetables for summer salads and to can for the winter and sun-loving daisies to grace the kitchen table. Shovels and a coil of barbed wire stood in the corner—Papa intended to begin stringing a fence around at least part of the property. The barn was fuller than Sarah remembered. Most of the newer items in the barn had come on the stagecoach.

She filled a wood bucket with corn, turning the handle on the silo to let the kernels run out. Then she broke off four sheaves of rich, bright green alfalfa hay and carried them out to Moon Dancer.

The pinto waited for her at the gate to the corral, his head high as he sniffed the air. Sarah smiled with excitement and pride—this was her horse! *He's the one I've looked for,* she thought as she tossed the hay on the ground and set the bucket down for him. The other horse had been let out to forage, but Sarah had no intention of letting Moon Dancer out until she was sure he knew this was home.

Moon Dancer plowed into the bucket of corn, gulping down bite after bite. Sarah checked that the pail in the corral still held water so that he could wash all his food down. "I imagine you're hungry after your travels," Sarah said, resting her foot on the bottom rail of the fence as she watched the pinto eat. "I wonder where you've been?"

She might have a better idea after she rode him. Sarah hurried up to the house for breakfast, a skip in her step, happier than she could ever remember being. Here it was her birthday, she had found a wonderful horse, and Papa wasn't mad at her. Once Sarah showed that Moon Dancer was ridable, Papa would be sure to let her keep him.

"We'll open presents tonight, when Papa finishes up with the branding," Mama said, turning from the big iron cookstove as Sarah came in the kitchen door and putting a basket of fresh-baked biscuits on the table. "Does he need you to help him today, Sarah?"

"I don't know. I'll ask." Sarah sat at the table, where Rachel was already devouring bacon and eggs, her face almost touching her plate. Sarah doubted if she would be needed to help with the branding with all those hands around. And since Mama seemed well enough today to cook for everybody, Sarah might not be needed around the house, either.

Since Sarah had arrived at the ranch, she'd helped Papa with a lot of tasks—with Mama so often ill, he'd had no one else to turn to. A week ago Sarah had sat for hours far out on the range in the freezing nighttime cold with a weak orphan calf, trying to get it to drink milk from her fingers. When she couldn't feel her fingers anymore, Papa had taken over the calf while Sarah split wood with an ax for the kitchen fire. She'd been rewarded when, after two days, the calf learned to drink milk from a pail. Now he was a big, sturdy fellow, and she couldn't tell anything had ever been wrong with him.

"The stage is due today. You should meet it." Mama gave her a secret smile, brushing off her biscuit-floured hands. "I think something for you might be aboard."

"I guess I'll have to wait until Papa can spare time from the branding," Sarah said, reaching for a biscuit in the basket and quickly buttering it. Driving the horse and wagon the ten miles to the stagecoach stop was one of the few things Papa wouldn't let her do by herself.

Sarah ate several biscuits and a piece of bacon, then excused herself and returned to her bedroom. In the corner closest to her bed, resting on a pine sawhorse, was her sidesaddle, the soft, burnished black leather gleaming in the muted light. Sarah kept the saddle in her room instead of in the barn to keep it clean. "I haven't ridden sidesaddle since Fort Smith," she murmured, running her fingers over the saddle's sleek seat. When she'd tried out the ranch horses last fall, seeking a mount, she'd ridden astride in big Western cowboy saddles. The saddles were beautiful—the leather tooled with floral patterns, animals, or even a campfire scene from cowboy life—but the saddles had seemed so heavy and cumbersome, not what she wanted for a light-stepping horse like Moon Dancer. *A refined saddle for a refined horse,* she told herself as she hefted the sidesaddle.

Slipping quickly through the kitchen, which was now empty, Sarah returned to the barn to select a bridle. She scanned the row of bridles hanging on the wall. They all had different kinds of bits. Sarah had always ridden her father's horses with snaffle bits, two simple attached iron bars, but she knew a snaffle was a mild bit. The cowboys rode their horses with bits that had a big upright bend in the middle—that was called a high-port bit, and it painfully struck the top of the horse's mouth when the reins were pulled, forcing the horse to mind. Sarah didn't want to hurt Moon Dancer, but she did want to be able to get his attention. She chose a medium-port bit and attached it with strips of rawhide to a black headstall, the straight piece of leather that went behind the horse's ears and held the bit. *Black saddle, black bridle, black-and-white pinto,* she thought with satisfaction. *It all matches.*

At the corral, Moon Dancer had finished all his hay and grain and was waiting for her again, his head stuck over the top rail of the fence. "Did you have a good breakfast?" Sarah asked. "I guess so, since not a crumb is left."

The pinto eyed the saddle, but he didn't move off. Sarah took that as another sign that he'd been ridden before. She'd forgotten to bring a halter to tie him up with, but Moon Dancer stood quietly while she threw her thick, fluffy white saddle pad over his back, then the saddle itself. He didn't even move when she tightened the girth.

"You're definitely trained," Sarah said, casting a quick look over her shoulder. She counted on Papa's being too busy with the branding to observe her from the big corral, but if he did find out she'd ridden the horse, she could always say she'd tacked up Moon Dancer right under his nose—surely he'd seen her—and so she thought he'd be fine with her going for a ride.

Next she bridled the pinto, pulling the headstall over his ears. Moon Dancer rubbed his head against her hands affectionately, gently swishing his tail. Sarah gathered the reins under his chin and eased back the boards of the corral gate. She didn't want to mount up in plain sight of Papa and the hands. As she led the pinto toward the house, Sarah made a quick calculation of where Mama would be. Midmorning—she would probably be tending to the lunchtime cooking. With any luck, she wouldn't look out the kitchen window and see Sarah and her saddled horse going by. Sarah didn't especially want to run into Rachel, either, who would want to tag along and might blurt Sarah's doings to Mama or Papa, but there was no telling where Rachel might be—she could be out with the chickens, playing with her dolls in the house, or any number of places.

Sarah increased her pace to almost a run, and Moon Dancer trotted behind her. They passed a pile of lumber at the front of the house that Papa was intending to use for a front porch, then the grainy, mud-colored adobe walls at the side and back of the house. Sarah tugged at the reins to stop Moon Dancer, then took a deep breath.

Out here, it was completely still. Sarah looked down to the river, a glittering string of pools joined by sandbars, and at the welcome cool of the willows, barely leafed out with new spring growth, overhanging the river on both sides. Beyond the short patch of green she could see the desert, an endless stretch of beige sand, dotted by the dark green of spiny yucca and thick-armed cholla cactus. In the far distance, fifteen miles away, she could see towering Cooke's Peak. The stage would come from that direction, through Cooke's Canyon. That was where so many Apache ambushes had been.

Moon Dancer stepped forward and looked in the direction

of the river too, his ears pricked.

"What's out there?" Sarah asked him, patting his neck. "Nothing, looks like to me. So where did you come from?"

From right below Cooke's Peak, Sarah thought she saw a cloud of dust—but it could have just been the wavering of the horizon in the heat. She shook her head and lowered the saddle's stirrup. She needed to get on with her ride before someone discovered her.

The sidesaddle stirrup was on one side, hanging down just like on a man's saddle, but instead of a stirrup on the other side, the sidesaddle had thick pommels to hold the rider's leg in place above the stirrup. Sidesaddles were both very comfortable and elegant, Sarah thought, swinging on top of the saddle with practiced ease. *I must look pretty as a picture,* she thought with satisfaction as she gathered her reins, adjusting the length in her hands so that she had light contact with the bit. She had a brief, unsettling moment as Moon Dancer crab-stepped sideways, but she reminded herself that he almost certainly wasn't used to the sidesaddle style of riding, with more weight on one side. Sarah gave a short tug on the reins, and after a moment he stopped misbehaving and stood still.

Sarah settled her feet in the saddle and looked around again. "Where shall we go?" she asked her horse. A thrill went through Sarah at her words. She'd lived in this country since last fall, but never had she seen it like this, from the back of her own horse. From high up, the endless miles of flat sand, the low ranch buildings, and the twinkling river pools lay at her feet, and she was part of the clear, boundless blue sky, queen of it all. *How very different from last night,* Sarah thought, *when I found the land so frightening.* The daylit desert was stark, open, and inviting. Her heart beating quickly with joy, Sarah smiled as a jackrabbit, long ears waggling, hopped across the sand and hid behind a rock.

"At last I have found a horse," she whispered, touching her fingertips to Moon Dancer's black mane. "And you are everything I wanted you to be."

Sarah leaned forward, easing Moon Dancer into a walk. *I think I'll ride over to the Stautons' and show them my horse,* she thought. The Stautons were the Chiltons' nearest neighbors, although Sarah couldn't see the ranch, eight miles distant, from here. Mr. Stauton and his oldest son, Calvin, would be coming over to the Chiltons' when they finished their own chores to help with the branding again, but thirteen-year-old Phoebe would be back at home. Phoebe's family had lived on their ranch for three years, having come all the way from Pittsburgh, Pennsylvania. Like everybody else for a hundred miles square, they were delighted that Mr. Chilton was a doctor. Until he'd moved here, the ranch families had relied solely on home remedies.

Sarah gingerly rode Moon Dancer well out into the desert, taking care to keep him at a walk or slow trot. She was confident in her horsemanship, but this was a brand-new mount. She intended to take it easy on their first ride and stay far from the ranch. That way if she and the pinto had any disagreements, her father wouldn't be witness to them.

Sarah remembered that Moon Dancer was almost certainly a Western-broke horse—that meant he neck-reined, or turned in response to a touch on his neck with the reins, instead of turning to a direct pull on one of the reins, as in English riding. Sarah carefully touched Moon Dancer's neck with one of the reins. After a moment the pinto changed direction, moving away from the pressure.

A little slow, but not too bad, she thought, a smile spreading across her face again.

She saw movement at the horizon, wavering in the shimmers

of heat that already rose from the desert. It was a group of animals, moving toward her. For a moment she was frightened, but then she saw that it was just a large herd of pronghorn antelope. They were traveling upwind and had not yet seen her.

Moon Dancer had seen them too.

The antelope stopped, turning their black faces and curly horns in Sarah's direction. They were so close, she could see the golden brown of their coats, shading into white undersides, and their black noses, rapidly sniffing the wind.

Suddenly the antelope broke and fled, a perfect oval of cloven hooves kicking up sand and dust.

Moon Dancer's going to spook, Sarah thought rapidly. Instinctively she gripped the reins tighter in one hand and grabbed the pommel of the sidesaddle to prepare herself.

The next second Moon Dancer bolted, jarring Sarah almost out of the saddle. But to Sarah's amazement he ran *after* the herd, not *away* from it.

What had gotten into him? Her teeth rattling, her bones aching as she bounced on the saddle with each leap, Sarah could hardly believe the pinto's speed—he was closing on the herd. But she knew she didn't stand a chance of staying with him. She couldn't get her balance well enough to even pull back on his head, and at every bounce she was closer to losing her stirrup. "I've—got—to—get—off," she whispered, her eyes frantically casting over the terrain for a soft spot, but all she saw was scattered rocks and the pointy green spines of yucca. The ground was rushing by so fast, it was a tan blur.

Ahead she saw an arroyo—a broad crack in the earth several feet across. During the rare desert rains, arroyos filled up with water. This one was bone dry. As Moon Dancer closed on it, his hooves kicking up clouds of sand as he raced even faster, Sarah barely managed not to scream with fright. She tried to grip the saddle even tighter with her hand to prepare herself for the impact of a jump or a scramble. Without slowing, Moon Dancer took a great leap over the deep, broken ground.

Hot air rushed by Sarah's ears. She tried to stay with the horse, but she could feel herself flying up, then out of the saddle, arms flailing. *At least I've lost my stirrup and won't be dragged,* she had time to think, then the ground slammed into her.

6

For several seconds Sarah just lay there. She was afraid to move and find out how badly hurt she was. Her head ached from hitting the ground so hard, and her whole body was throbbing. "What if I've broken a bone?" she whispered. Although her father could likely set it, she wouldn't be able to do chores for weeks—maybe months. How would Papa manage without her?

Determinedly Sarah forced herself to sit up. She had landed in a clear patch of sand, right in front of a huge black-and-gray boulder that could have broken her skull. Sarah shuddered, her body trembling from shock and pain. Gingerly she moved both of her legs under her dusty skirt. They seemed to be all right. But her head . . . Sarah lifted a hand to it and cried out with pain. Her left arm hurt excruciatingly.

Sarah dropped her head, waiting for the dizziness to pass. Then she looked over her arm, without trying to move it again. Her blue bodice was ripped at the elbow, and blood stained the cloth just above. Gritting her teeth, Sarah pulled up the shirt-sleeve at the rip and looked again at her arm, expecting to see protruding bone and ragged flesh. She let out a weary breath of relief. Not too bad. Just a really awful scrape. She must have just glanced her arm against the rock when she fell.

Sarah shoved her hair out of her eyes with her right hand. So if she wasn't badly injured, she had to get home. Where was Moon Dancer?

Tears blurred Sarah's eyes. "He's gone," she whispered. "This is the worst of the things I've done—I've let him get away. How could I be so irresponsible?"

Sarah jerked herself to her feet, holding on to the big rock, which she now saw was marked with her blood. The least she could do was get herself home, before Mama and everyone else missed her and worried to death.

Before starting out, Sarah carefully checked the direction. She thought she'd ridden only a mile or two, but the desert looked the same everywhere. Squinting, she glanced up at the sun, now almost overhead. She needed to turn straight around and keep the sun to her right. That was the way back to the ranch.

As she walked, Sarah kept her eyes on the ground, watching where she stepped. She didn't want to disturb a rattlesnake or plant one of her feet, in their thin leather boots, on a horse-crippler cactus. By now the sun . . . Sarah realized that her bonnet had flown off on her wild ride. *I must be getting even more suntanned or burned,* Sarah thought unhappily. *No need to fear the Indians—they will mistake me for one of their own.* Mama would be so dismayed when Sarah showed up with her complexion ruined.

Sarah saw a small dust cloud up ahead. *Apaches?* she wondered. But she was almost too dispirited to care. Besides, it was a very small dust cloud. And now that she looked harder, Sarah realized that it stretched back a long way—almost to her.

"It's Moon Dancer! He's going home!" Sarah laughed aloud, a smile breaking through her tears. Suddenly she had a whole new perspective on her ride. Moon Dancer had run home, and so she would have another chance with him. Now she just needed to get home herself and wash up before anyone saw her. Perhaps then Papa would think the horse had just broken free and wouldn't even realize she'd tried to ride him—she could say she'd just been fitting the saddle.

After almost an hour of walking, forcing herself to keep up a good pace despite her near exhaustion and thirst from the burning sun, Sarah reached the ranch house. No one was in sight, except for the men working at the big corral. Sarah sneaked around the side of the house, hoping to get to the pump before anyone saw her. She knew she must look a sight. The ripped sleeve of her dress was thoroughly soaked with blood, her skirt was streaked with dirt, and her lips tasted gritty. Her hair, fallen out of its braid and hanging in her eyes, was past praying for.

She reached the pump and hastily swung the handle. A blessed shower of water blasted out of the faucet, spattering her dusty boots. Sarah quickly stuck her hands under the stream and splashed water on her hot, sunburned face.

"I put the pinto in the small corral again." Papa's voice came from behind her. "I was just about to ride out looking for you, but then I saw you walking up under your own steam."

Sarah quickly turned, but water running into her eyes almost blinded her. Papa was sure to be furious with her for her recklessness. Oddly, though, his voice was quiet, although he was swatting his cowboy hat against his knee.

"Your mother—" Papa fell silent. "I can't have you getting hurt or killed."

Sarah sucked in a quick breath and rubbed her eyes. Papa was staring at his boots, his shoulders sagging. *He's so worried about Mama,* she thought. *Does he think she's going to die having this baby?* A sick feeling filled Sarah's stomach. Mama had already lost three baby boys, two between Sarah and Rachel and another just a year ago. None of Papa's tonics had ever made Mama any stronger.

"And I simply cannot watch you every minute," Papa continued, his voice still quiet.

Sarah swallowed hard, licking her parched lips. She feared what Papa's next words would be—she couldn't imagine he would let her keep the horse after this escapade. "I—I know, Papa," she said. "I—"

Her father shook his head. "Sarah, I don't think there's much hope for that bronc."

"Yes, there is!" Sarah cried. She didn't know exactly what had gone wrong on their ride, but she was sure she could fix it. After all, how often would she run into a herd of antelope? Papa was always talking about how big game was getting scarce with all the new settlers. "You should have seen how he went before he spooked," she added.

"Give him to the cowboys," her father snapped. "That's all he's good for."

"You said he was my birthday horse!" Sarah said frantically.

Papa ran his hand through his hair, then jammed his cowboy hat back on his head. "I must get back to work, Sarah."

Sarah tried to calm herself. Papa hadn't said he would definitely get rid of Moon Dancer, and he had even put him in the corral for her. *The next ride will be better—I'll stay in the corral,* she told herself. *And I'll use a cowboy saddle.* Although it might not be ladylike or even civilized, Sarah realized that she had no chance in a sidesaddle of riding out another fit like Moon Dancer'd had.

Papa swung around and glared at her. "Change your clothes before your mother sees you," he barked. "Don't upset her."

"I won't," Sarah said, starting for the house. She was anxious to get out of her tattered, bloodstained dress herself. As she turned, Sarah caught sight of a faint, distant cloud of dust to the northeast.

"Papa, look! Isn't that the stage?" she called.

Papa stopped. "Looks that way," he said after a moment.

"Can we go meet it?" Sarah asked. *Maybe that will take his mind off Mama's illness, my wounds, and getting rid of Moon Dancer,* she thought. *Besides, my birthday present is there!*

"All right," Papa said tersely. "I'm hoping some more wire I ordered for fences will be aboard. Get cleaned up and find your sister—she won't want to miss the trip. And don't bother your mother about any of this."

"Yes, Papa," Sarah said, trying to keep back tears. Papa's tone was so harsh. After her mistakes with Moon Dancer, she wondered if he'd ever trust her again.

The house was still quiet—Mama must be resting after serving lunch to the hands. Trying to be soundless, Sarah tiptoed into her parents' bedroom and dug through the rag bag Mama kept in a corner of the room. Sarah needed to find a bandage so that fresh bleeding from her arm didn't ruin another dress. She glanced at the scrape, then looked away—the sight of it made her queasy. It was about three inches long and two inches wide, and it was still seeping blood.

Mama was sleeping on her side, her beautiful, unlined face relaxed. Sarah let out a short sigh of relief. They just had to get Mama through having the baby, then she should be all right. Mama seemed fine now—maybe she was over the worst of her trouble and wouldn't have any more bad days. Mama'd said that was how it sometimes worked out with babies.

In her own room, Sarah tied the cloth around her scrape, using her right hand and her teeth to pull the knot tight. She quickly changed into a clean dark brown dress and hurried over to the mirror to brush out her tangled hair. Papa was likely fit to be tied from waiting on her for so long.

"Now I'm myself again," she murmured as she plaited the blond strands back into braids. "Except . . ."

Sarah stared at herself in the mirror, disturbed. Her face was deeply tanned, and a smattering of freckles bridged her nose. Her blond hair had pale, almost white streaks in it. Last night she'd enjoyed her wild look, but she didn't want it to become a habit.

"Sarah!" Papa shouted.

Grabbing a broad-brimmed straw hat from a hook above the chest, Sarah ran outside. *I'll be careful to wear a hat from now on,* she thought, tying the ribbons under her chin. *That should lighten the freckles.*

She had no time to check on Moon Dancer, but Sarah noticed as she hurried to the wagon that the pail of water she had set inside the corral had been replaced by one of the metal watering troughs. If Papa was helping her take care of the horse, that must mean he hadn't given up on her and Moon Dancer completely, she hoped.

Sarah climbed up onto the wagon seat beside Papa and Rachel and folded her long skirt beneath her. Papa clucked to the cart horse, a bay that he'd bought cheap from a couple of silver miners gone bust who had returned back east. With a groan, the spoked wood wheels began to turn, sinking a little into the sand. Sarah grabbed the side of the seat to steady herself. "Hang on to me, Rachel," she instructed, and her little sister slipped her small hand into Sarah's.

The girls smiled at each other—going to the stage stop was a very special treat, the only time they got new, storebought goods. Sarah had once been to the bustling mining town of Silver City, only about a day's wagon ride distant, but the stores there seemed to sell only flannel shirts, coffee, pickaxes, and other mining supplies. The stage brought fancy, fine goods from back east when folks ordered them—on the last trip Sarah had gotten an exquisite tortoiseshell hair comb and Mama a box of sequins and a shimmering length of yellow ribbon to use in dressmaking. On one stage trip even Rachel's prize bantam rooster had bumped his way here from Fort Smith.

I can't wait to get my birthday present! Sarah thought, so excited, she wanted to run the ten miles to the stage stop ahead of the wagon.

Her happiness making her bold, Sarah leaned across Rachel. "Papa, what should I feed Moon Dancer?" she asked.

"What did you feed him?" Papa kept his eyes straight ahead on the faint wagon ruts leading to the stage stop. "He seems pretty lively."

"Hay and corn," Sarah said tentatively. She knew she must have done something wrong for Moon Dancer to act that way, but she couldn't think what. She'd given the pinto the best feed they had.

"What kind of hay? How much did you feed him?" her father pressed.

"I took the alfalfa—we had the most of that. I gave him four sheaves of alfalfa and half a bucket of corn for breakfast," Sarah said uncertainly.

Her father sighed sharply. "Sarah, either one of those fed in quantity would make even a tame beast go wild."

"Well, what should I have done?" Sarah asked timidly.

"Turn him out to graze," Papa said shortly, but he didn't seem too angry. "He should do fine on the ranch grass."

"I will," Sarah said tentatively, starting to smile. Moon Dancer would get another chance!

Rachel squeezed her hand. "You can keep him forever!" she said into Sarah's ear.

Sarah nodded, hoping Papa wouldn't hear. She didn't want to press the matter of the horse with him too far just yet.

After over two hours of rattling and jouncing on the wagon, Sarah saw the stage stop up ahead, at first just a wavering mirage in the dust and heat, then slowly forming into the high adobe walls of the corral surrounding the buildings. The stage was approaching the stop rapidly from the east in a huge, swirling cloud of dust. *I'm exactly on time to get my present!* Sarah thought, grabbing Rachel's skirt as her little sister tried to jump up and forcing her to stay seated. Rachel clapped, then waved to the stage.

Papa pulled up the team just outside the high wood gate. Just behind it was a combination hotel and store. At the front of the structure was a storeroom for goods, and in back were large, comfortable rooms rented out to travelers. The gate was open now, awaiting the stage.

Sarah hopped down from the wagon, then tried to brush the dust off her skirt. But the fine particles clung stubbornly, turning her brown dress the color of rust. *No matter,* Sarah told herself. The stage passengers and everyone meeting the stage would be just as dusty.

Now that it was closer, Sarah could see the stage emerging from its high, roiling cloud of dust. A team of twelve mules was hitched in pairs to a square coach, with luggage, boxes, and sacks strapped on top. The stage had two windows on the side, but they appeared to be shuttered or curtained—Sarah couldn't see any passengers looking out. Two drivers sat on the broad wood top seat.

Sarah smiled, shielding her eyes from the sun with her hand. "I can't wait to see the treasures aboard!" she called to Papa.

He yelled something back, but Sarah couldn't hear it over

the creaking of the swaying stage and the pounding of the mules' hooves. Now that the stage was within five hundred yards of the stop, Sarah could see that one of the drivers was leaning forward, lashing the mules with a long whip. The other driver was twisted around backward, a rifle pointed at the dust.

Crack! Sarah flinched. *He's shot at something!* she realized.

The lead two mules' eyes were wild with terror, rolling white, and lather frothed on their sweat-darkened necks. The whole team was running flat out, their legs eating up the ground in a frantic blur of speed.

"Something's wrong!" Sarah cried.

Papa roughly grabbed her shoulder and spun her around. "Run!" he shouted. "Don't stop! Get inside!"

Sarah raced through the gate, choking on dust, barely able to see Papa and Rachel in front of her. They had time only to flatten themselves against the wall behind the gate before the stage roared through the opening. Three burly men slammed the heavy gate closed while one of the stage drivers hauled back on the high-stepping, snorting mules' reins, trying to stop the excited animals before they plunged clean through the other end of the corral.

"Papa, what's happened?" Sarah whispered. The stage had never before arrived in such a state.

"Apache attack," Papa said shortly.

The stage driver had managed to turn the mule team and brought the stage back up to the gate. He pulled the team to a halt, and four passengers, three men and a woman, climbed out the door. One of the passengers, an older man with a bushy gray beard, was clutching a Bible in one hand and a bowler hat in the other and mumbling. All of the passengers looked white even under the thick layer of dust that coated them from their heads to their shoes. Sarah had never in her life seen people look so frightened. The woman passenger, who wore a dark, well-cut dress and had the respectable look of a schoolteacher, was trembling so much, she could hardly stand. The other two male passengers were holding her up.

How very deadly these Apaches must be if they can so frighten people, Sarah thought.

The innkeeper, a tall, gracious, white-haired woman, hurried over to the passengers. "Come," she said, gesturing to the hotel. "Let's get you people settled. You'll all feel better after you've had a bite to eat."

As the passengers stumbled off with the innkeeper, the two stage drivers climbed down from the box. The shorter of the two set his rifle up on the box and looked back at the gate. Sarah listened nervously, but she couldn't hear anything except the occasional stomp of the mules' hooves. The innkeeper's two oldest sons stepped up to the mules and began to unharness them.

"Those damned Apaches are gone," said the other driver, a skinny man with a weathered tan face. "We outran them this time."

Sarah stared in horror at two long, feathered arrows quivering in the side of the stage. The arrowheads were buried deep in the wood.

"Bullet holes too, miss," said the thin driver, following her gaze. He pointed to a smattering of half-inch holes across the coach door. "They really let us have it. Don't know how nobody was hurt or killed."

"How did you fight them off?" Papa asked. His expression was grave.

Sarah hoped the drivers would tell the whole story of the Apache attack. They didn't seem as petrified as the passengers.

"Those Indians rode up behind us—they came out of nowhere, like they always do, as we went through Cooke's Canyon," the thin driver went on, sitting on the passenger step into the stage. He took off his hat and wiped sweat from his face with a red handkerchief. "One of them jumped on top of the stage, even though we were going full speed. His partner kept his horse running alongside and caught the things he threw down. I was waiting every second for him to swing down into the coach and scalp everybody."

Sarah felt a quick clutch of fear grab her shoulders. She was glad to see that Rachel had wandered over to one of the innkeeper's young grandchildren and was playing marbles in front of the store. This story could give her nightmares.

"The one that stayed on his horse shot the rifle out of my hands before I even saw him," the short driver said, sounding frustrated. "I had a spare under the seat, but it took me a minute to grab it and cock it. We were going so fast, the coach was rocking like it was about to turn over. I don't know if they followed us all the way here or not—I kept shooting just in case they did."

"The shots drove them off," said the other driver. "Think we saved most of the load."

"We saved our *lives.*" The short driver spat at the ground. "And the passengers are still breathing."

"Sarah." Papa's voice was behind her. "We must get back to the ranch. Although the hands are still there, with Apaches marauding . . ."

Sarah turned quickly to him with frightened eyes. *Mama!*

"It's all right, daughter," Papa said gently. "The cowboys are armed and know well the dangers of Apaches. But I will be asking you to keep a sharp lookout on the drive home. Let's get your birthday present from the stage and go."

"And what might the little lady's present be?" the short driver asked, managing a smile.

"I know just what it is." Papa swung up onto the driver's seat of the stage and looked under the canvas covering on top used to protect the more fragile freight.

Sarah felt her shoulders relaxing, and a smile crept across her face. No one had been killed or even hurt, and now she would get her special birthday present from home!

"If you're looking for that bolt of pretty daisy-patterned cloth, it ain't there." The skinny driver sighed. "Those Indians are plain crazy—that was the first thing one grabbed while he was poking through the goods. Guess it caught his eye."

"I'm sorry, sweetheart," Papa said, his forehead wrinkling with concern. "But I'll order another bolt of cloth to be delivered on the next stage—the Apaches surely won't raid again so soon."

Sarah felt so sick to her stomach, she thought she'd faint. Unable to speak, she shook her head and leaned heavily against one of the stage's tall wood wheels. How could those Indians take her birthday present? She could have made a pretty new dress with Mama, to wear on special occasions and to brighten her mother's spirits. But now she had nothing to help Mama and nothing for herself. Her birthday was utterly ruined.

Those Apaches are frightful, beastly savages, she thought, closing her eyes and trying not to cry. But she could feel the tears spilling over her lashes.

"Sarah—come. We must get back to the ranch," Papa said, touching her hand.

Sarah straightened her back and wiped her eyes on her sleeve. One thing she could do for Mama was return quickly to her. "Rachel, we're leaving," she called, stretching out her hand to her little sister.

Rachel ran over, kicking up a small dust cloud with her boots. Sarah stared at her, frozen.

She had just remembered the dust cloud she'd seen that morning right before she set out to ride Moon Dancer. It had been a wide plume on the horizon, in the direction of Cooke's Peak.

Sarah stifled a gasp. She realized now, with terrible fear, that while she had been out in that desert alone, raising her own very visible cloud of dust, a few miles away a band of Apaches had been riding to attack, rob, and murder.

7

“**Move that jump a little farther out**,” Sarah directed her friend Phoebe Stauton. Sarah sat back in Moon Dancer’s saddle, gathered her reins in one hand, and pointed where she thought the fifth jump on her course should go. “Moon popped it the last time—if he has to fit another stride in there, he should take a nice jump.”

Phoebe obligingly dragged back the two mesquite stumps, which Sarah’s father had dug out of the cornfield, and rested the long, thin cottonwood pole on top of them again. “That good?” she asked, brushing her red curls out of her face. Phoebe pushed her cowboy hat down harder on her head and squinted up at Sarah. The flood of morning light cascaded around them, causing a broken iron hoe, a gray rock, and the coat of a large, curious calf to burst into sparkles.

“Perfect.” Sarah looked around the course one last time. She had set up the jumps in a rough circle, with about the same distance between each one. They were all about two feet high, with mesquite stumps, buckets, and even part of a broken plow to hold the crossbars up. She and Phoebe had put the jumps at the back of the ranch house, out of sight of the kitchen and corrals. Although Sarah had owned Moon Dancer for two months now, when she started jumping him three weeks ago, she hadn't been too sure how he would do, and she was ever mindful of Papa's reaction to riding disasters. Luckily Moon Dancer was a natural jumper—he had sailed over the course with ease the first time she tried him.

Sarah slid her boots back a bit in the big, rawhide Western stirrups, positioning them carefully on the balls of her feet. "Ready, Moon?" she asked.

The pinto lightly pawed the ground, eager to be off. Sarah rubbed his neck to calm him a little. Certainly Moon Dancer had no problem with energy. But after he had run off with her on that first ride, Sarah had ridden him in the big corral, then just around the ranch, sticking close to the buildings, working on control of his speed and movements. After the Apache scare at the stage stop, she couldn't take him out in the open desert anyway. Sarah had taught Moon Dancer that when she sat back, he was to stop. It wasn't too hard—she just pointed him at the wall of the house and sat back the moment he had to stop to avoid the wall. Most of the time he listened.

Moon Dancer's large eyes were roving over the jumps too. He learned quickly, and she was sure he was planning how he would approach the course.

"Shouldn't you have a band playing for your show?" Calvin Stauton asked, sauntering over. At fifteen, he counted himself a grown man. He wore the usual cowboy getup of worn work shirt, blue neckerchief, straw cowboy hat, black chaps, and down-at-the-heel tan cowboy boots.

"Shouldn't you be working?" Phoebe asked, frowning. Calvin had ridden in from the range about an hour ago with one of the other neighbors. They had been helping round up a stray herd of the Chiltons' cattle. Sarah's father didn't go with them since he didn't want to leave the ranch unprotected.

"We do not need a band," Sarah said coldly. *I'll show him how jumping is done,* she thought, tightening her cowboy hat under her chin. Although she still didn't like the way she looked in cowboy dress, she had come to appreciate its uses—her freckles had faded.

Sarah had become accustomed to an audience when she rode her horse. Last week she had attempted to teach Moon Dancer basic dressage, including the side pass, where the horse elegantly crossed his legs to move on a diagonal. Calvin had been on hand to laugh then, too. Still, Sarah was sure Calvin understood what she was doing. Although the cowboys didn't teach their horses to do the side pass, control and precision were important in the training of any horse.

As Sarah looked out over the mismatched course, she couldn't help remembering the elegant designer courses, with their red-and-white-striped poles and flower arrangements, that she used to ride over in Fort Smith. *This serves the purpose,* she told herself firmly, and aimed Moon Dancer at the first jump. The two cottonwood branches were in the shape of an X, but because little twigs sprouted all over the branches, the jump was really a cross between an X and a brush jump.

Moon Dancer needed no urging to begin the course. He flew from a standstill into a gallop and crossed the distance to the first jump in three strides. With difficulty Sarah leaned forward in the Western saddle—the horn got in the way—but Moon Dancer didn't seem to need her help. He powered over the jump with two feet to spare. Sarah pointed him at the next jump. Moon Dancer fought her just a little, yanking his head around and trying to run out. He definitely had his own opinions, but Sarah pulled him firmly back to face a row of buckets. Moon Dancer tossed his head but settled down to the task, taking a nice jump. She finished the course and pulled him up in front of Phoebe and Calvin, smiling. "You're such a wonderful horse, Moon Dancer," she whispered, leaning over his neck. "You're willing, smart, and beautiful—all the horse I ever wanted."

"Can I try riding him?" Phoebe asked.

Sarah hesitated. "All right," she said. "But try him in the corral first. He's got a lot of pep." Sarah wasn't sure how much riding experience Phoebe had. The girls didn't see each other that much because of the difficulty in getting from one ranch to the other.

"Calvin!" Mrs. Stauton called from the ranch house. Sarah was glad Mrs. Staunton had come over because Mama was feeling a bit poorly today, and Mrs. Stauton had made her a cup of tea and was providing company, catching Mama up on the goings-on at the Stautons' ranch and Silver City. Sarah didn't know if Mama could possibly be interested in news of a silver strike, but at least the chat was taking her mind off her sickness.

Calvin saluted the girls. "See you later," he said, and walked toward the house, spurs jingling. "Oh, Phoebe?" he called over his shoulder. "When we're home, you need to help me fix the barn wall—that last rainstorm caved the adobe in."

Phoebe made a face, but she yelled back, "Okay!" Both girls knew that they were required to help with any chore that needed doing, even if in Fort Smith and Pittsburgh those chores might have been considered men's work. Sometimes the chores could be overwhelming.

At least I get to ride Moon Dancer almost every day, Sarah thought as she led him to the corral. She knew Papa wanted her to have fun, but he also thought having another well-broke horse around the ranch was a worthwhile undertaking.

Sarah removed the board gate, positioned Moon Dancer in the center of the corral, and adjusted the stirrups for Phoebe's shorter legs. "How much have you ridden?" she asked the younger girl.

"Not a whole lot. We don't even own a broke horse now—our cart horse died, and that's why your papa had to drive us over here in your wagon. Calvin's riding some half-broke bronc he got from a miner passing through to California—that horse throws him as much as it lets him ride it."

"Well, start off slow and see how he does." Sarah watched critically as Phoebe awkwardly stuck her foot in the left stirrup and hoisted herself onto Moon Dancer's back.

Phoebe was slouching in the saddle, shoulders forward, heels up. Sarah frowned but didn't say anything. She knew Phoebe had to get her bearings before she could work on her posture. But the other girl obviously hadn't ridden much. Sarah hoped her horse would behave and not show his wild side.

Moon Dancer circled the corral at a slow walk, his head down, neck relaxed. He seemed content to give a pony ride, as if he were at a county fair. Sarah could feel a smile curling her lips as she watched Moon Dancer's light, easy walk. He had become muscular over the last two months from the good feed and steady workouts. Papa said he was a young horse, so he might just be filling out as he grew up. Sarah was proud at how kind Moon Dancer was being to Phoebe.

Where's Rachel? Sarah wondered, glancing behind her. The ranch was completely still, except for the occasional buzz of a darting fly. *She should work on her riding too.* But Rachel had zero interest in horses. Sarah doubted if she could even find her little sister. Rachel had any number of spots she could disappear to on the ranch.

The sun pounded Sarah's shoulders, so strong it was like two fists. "Let's go in," she called to Phoebe.

"I wouldn't mind a glass of iced tea," Phoebe said, halting Moon Dancer in front of Sarah. Phoebe rubbed Moon Dancer's sleek shoulder and carefully climbed out of the saddle. "He was a good boy."

Moon Dancer nudged Phoebe, and Sarah handed her a young carrot from the garden to give him as a treat. Then she unsaddled the pinto, brushed him down, and opened the corral for him. Moon Dancer shook himself hard, his black mane flying every which way. Then he looked quickly around, trotted out of the corral, and headed across the sandy yard to the river. Sarah knew that the other horse and cattle were probably down there, under the green patch of trees, standing in the cool mud. She couldn't help but worry, though, when Moon Dancer was loose, with the whole world around him for roaming. He seemed to know that the ranch was his home now, but Sarah hoped that he didn't stray again.

She and Phoebe trudged over to the house. "It's *hot*," Sarah complained.

Phoebe glanced at her, blue eyes round, and laughed outright. "You're joking. This is *April*! Wait till you see July around here. The temperature will be above a hundred every day. But don't worry—you'll get used to it. It's best to finish chores in the morning then, though."

Sarah rubbed her sweating forehead with her neckerchief. "I seriously doubt I will ever get used to heat like that," she said.

"You'd better," Phoebe replied. "I mean, what choice do you have?"

Sarah sighed. Lifting her skirt, she opened the wood door with her other hand and stepped into the kitchen.

Rachel sat at the table with Mama and Mrs. Stauton, eating a big, gooey slice of chocolate cake. The sun slanted through the west window, its dust-flecked beams turning the adobe room a warm gold. "There's a piece of cake for you," Rachel said to Sarah with her mouth full. "Mrs. Stauton brought it."

Sarah smiled her thanks, but she couldn't help remembering what a fine baker Mama was—when she could be on her feet long enough to do it. Mama specialized in pies: peach, apple, raspberry, and blueberry, with a light, buttery crust that no one in Fort Smith could imitate.

"We'd best be getting back." Mrs. Stauton rose from the table and looked at Mama, a crease between her brows. Mrs. Stauton was older than Mama, with streaks of white in her red hair, but Mrs. Stauton and Phoebe's plump pink cheeks and full figures were such a contrast to Mama's skin-and-bones body, except for the baby.

"Thank you kindly for coming." Mama smiled, her lovely face brightening, but she made no move to get up and show out her guests.

Sarah felt the familiar fear rising in her stomach. Mama had perfect manners, and she would be certain to accompany the Stautons to the door if she could get up at all. Today must be an even worse day for Mama than Sarah had realized. *I must help her as much as I can,* she thought.

"Rachel, please find Calvin and Papa," Sarah requested. "I'll start hitching up the wagon so that Papa can drive the Stautons home."

Mama leaned back in her chair. Her eyelids, white with red rims, fluttered closed.

"We'll come again very soon," said Mrs. Stauton gently. "It's good to see you, Elizabeth."

"And you as well." Mama smiled again, but she didn't open her eyes.

Please, God, let the baby come soon and release my mother from her pain, Sarah prayed as she followed Phoebe and her mother out of the kitchen.

The moon was moving at unnatural speed across the sky, swallowing the stars with its light. Was that the tail of a comet trailing behind the moon, cutting the wide, pale band of dawn?

Sarah sat up straight in her bed with a gasp, at first unable to tell if she dreamed still or was awake. The moon burst through her tiny window, glaring in the clear black sky, as strong as the desert sun.

Had the moon awoken her?

No. She'd heard a noise. Faint, but out of place among the chirp of an early cricket, the creak of the cottonwood branches by the river, Rachel's soft, rhythmic breaths. This was the sound of a horse's hooves, not random, as if the animal roamed, but steady and purposeful.

Sarah swung her feet over the side of the bed and hurried through the house, not stopping to dress. She threw open the front door and peered into the night. At first she couldn't make out anything, but then her eyes adjusted, and she could see the buildings' dark forms and their huge, manic shadows, distorted by the bright moon.

Something was moving by the small corral, where Sarah had put Moon Dancer up for the night. Sarah's breath caught in her throat. A dark shape was moving in the corral—it was Moon Dancer, but someone was riding him!

"Papa!" Sarah screamed. "Quick! Someone's stealing Moon Dancer!"

Her father ran out of the bedroom in his long johns, his rifle in one hand. He rushed by her out the door. Sarah ran after him, hardly aware of what she was doing. *My horse,* her heart, her whole body seemed to be crying out. *Don't take my horse!*

The sand spread under her bare feet, slowing her pace. As

she flailed along, she realized that to her right was another shape, but she had no time to worry about it.

Crack! A bullet whistled through the air.

Moon Dancer and his rider raced at the corral fence. "No!" Sarah whispered. Moon Dancer would crash through the boards and hurt himself terribly!

But just before he reached the fence, Moon Dancer lifted into the air. Dumbfounded, Sarah watched as he jumped the five-foot corral fence and landed with a thump on the other side.

The rider on Moon Dancer joined the other shadow and they rode off. Numb, Sarah noticed they were unbelievably good horsemen as they galloped bareback over the rough terrain of the desert.

Faint whoops floated back on the breeze, cries of triumph and joy. *Apaches,* she thought. A wave of terror rushed through her. Sarah sank to the ground, her legs suddenly too weak to hold her.

Papa walked over to her, lowering his rifle. "They took both of the horses," he said angrily. "They're gone, and I barely got off a shot."

Sarah stared out into the desert, willing her horse to come home, hating the thought of his strange, savage rider. *First my cloth, now my horse. Is there nothing they will not steal?* she thought. *Those things were mine by rights—they were my birthday presents.*

Papa held out his hand. "Come, child," he said. "I will report this to the army post in the morning."

"Do you think they can get Moon Dancer back?" Sarah cried, getting to her feet.

Papa said nothing. From his defeated look, Sarah knew he thought they'd never see the horses again.

A new feeling arose within her. As she and Papa walked to the house, Sarah began to shake, but not from cold or fright.

She was angry beyond compare, beyond anything she had ever felt. *How dare they take what I love!* she cried silently.

Rachel stood in the doorway, her face pale. "You need to come," she said. "Mama's very sick."

Mama screamed, a high, unearthly sound of pain. Pushing by Rachel, Sarah rushed back into the house. Her mother was in the kitchen, bent over, gripping the edge of the table. Papa grabbed her shoulders just as she was about to fall.

"Elizabeth?" he asked.

"It's . . . the baby. He's coming," Mama gasped.

"That can't be. It's too soon," Papa said desperately.

"I . . . know." Tears filled Mama's hazel eyes.

"We must get you to bed. Sarah, help me."

This cannot be happening again, Sarah thought. *Mama was so sure this baby would be all right!* Steadying Mama's light form by her elbows, Sarah and Papa slowly walked her back to the bedroom. After just a few steps Mama cried out and doubled over, clutching her stomach. Papa swept his arm under her and carried her to the bed.

Sarah stood outside the doorway, her eyes closed. *I will remain here and pray,* she thought. *Thankfully Papa is a doctor and can do what is needed.*

Mama's moans became louder and more agonized. "Sarah!" Papa called.

Sarah shook her head and gripped the door frame. "Don't make me go in there," she whispered.

Papa appeared in the doorway and took her arm. Sarah reluctantly looked at him. His eyes were panic stricken, almost crazed. A streak of bright red blood stained the front of his shirt, and there was more, darker blood on his hands. "The baby is coming for sure," he said. "But it's not only early, it's turned wrong in the womb. I need you to help me."

Sarah forced down the bile that was rising in her throat. *I have no choice,* she told herself.

"What can I do?" Rachel asked in a small voice. Sarah's sister stood behind her, blue eyes wide, her expression lost.

"Rachel—" Sarah did not know what to do with Rachel. "You will have to fetch us what we need," she said finally. "Can you do that for Mama?"

Rachel nodded. She seemed to feel a little better for having a task.

Mama screamed so loud, Sarah thought her mother must split in two. Hands trembling, Sarah followed Papa into the bedroom. *Dear God, don't let me see my mother die on this night,* she thought.

Hours later, Sarah stumbled out of the bedroom. She made her way to the rocking chair in the living room and pushed her untidy hair out of her eyes. For such a tiny baby, Zachary had taken a very long time to be born. He was beautiful, with big blue eyes, soft skin the color of a peach, and black fuzzy hair all over his tiny, smooth head. But Papa's hands were shaking as he placed the small baby in Mama's arms. The baby's cries were weak, and he was barely strong enough to nurse.

Mama is sick too, Sarah thought, dropping back her head. Mama almost couldn't stay awake to care for Zachary. Sarah could tell from the stunned, frightened expression in Papa's eyes that he expected the worst for both his wife and child.

I must look for Rachel, Sarah realized, rocking back upright. She couldn't remember when she had last seen her sister. Rachel had occasionally peeked into the sickroom, then ducked back out, like a scared yellow butterfly.

Sarah found Rachel in their bedroom, sound asleep on top of her quilt, her hands clasped under her head. Sarah sat down on Rachel's bed and stroked her sister's hair. *I can do nothing for her, either,* she thought. *It will break her heart if something should happen to Mama or the baby.* In that moment of sick helplessness, Sarah's anger returned.

"I hate those vicious Apaches!" she said aloud. Crossing swiftly to her bed, Sarah pulled her diary out from under her feather tick and took down her inkwell from the windowsill. The moon had passed over the house, and she couldn't see well enough to write. She returned to the living room and lit a fat tallow candle on the mantelpiece above the fireplace, then set the candle on the floor. Propping her back against the stone hearth, she turned to a fresh page in her diary and dipped her pen in the ink.

April 14, 1881

Dear Diary,

I do not know how to relate what has taken place this night. These events are too awful to bear, but I will try to put them down.

Mama has had the baby, but Papa says it is at least two months too soon. She will

Sarah stopped writing and set down her pen across the inkwell. She willed herself to stay composed. Gazing at the rocking chair across the room, Sarah wondered if Mama would ever sit in it again. When she lost the last baby, she was in bed for months. This time she seemed so much sicker.

Picking up her pen, Sarah bent over her page again. Sometimes writing helped her make sense of things. She could state very clearly what had happened, then perhaps she would see what to think, feel, and do.

Mama is very bad. She lost a lot of blood, and because the baby was turned wrong, the delivery was painful and strenuous. Papa did not wish me to see such disturbing sights, but I had to help him with the delivery, as there was no one else. I had much to do, keeping Mama's fever down with the application of cool cloths to her forehead and chest, boiling water for Papa's instruments, and comforting Mama in her agony. I even helped with the very moment of Zachary's birth and was the first to hold the treasure that is my little brother in my arms. I was not frightened then, only joyous. But I am frightened now.

Sarah sat quietly, tears on the edges of her eyelashes. If only she had her horse to cherish, to comfort her. "Moon Dancer," she whispered. "Where are you?"

She thought of the endless desert, the unending pattern of cactus and mesquite, sand and rock. Somewhere out there, her horse galloped under the moonlight with his strange, savage rider. Sarah dropped her pen, picked it up. Carefully she made her hand direct the pen into the inkwell so that she could write.

I must not give in to despair, although this night I have lost so much I hold dear, and our tragedy may not yet be at an end.

May God help us—and keep my horse safe from harm.

Part III

THE MEXICAN FRONTIER

8

Dark wind and darker sky, sky and wind, always faster, farther and away toward the mountain. A burst of cold, fresh air struck Bin-daa-dee-nin full in the face as he raced Moon That Flies across the hard desert sand, and the young Apache tipped back his head with a quiet cry. Then he bent low over the horse's neck, one shadow, moving effortlessly, guided by the full moon. Bin-daa-dee-nin balanced easily bareback, his strong legs gripping the horse's sweating sides while his hand steadied the deerskin bags of stolen food slung across Moon That Flies' neck. He and his horse had already traveled long, as the glowing eye of the moon sank toward the sand, putting ever more distance between themselves and the ranch, their lives and harm. But Moon That Flies, an Apache horse, was running tirelessly, endlessly over the desert: free, undefeated, master of his own body and spirit and of this land.

"My horse," Bin-daa-dee-nin whispered, letting his words be taken away into the desert and night, becoming a part of all and true. The horse's black-and-white shape melted into light and dark, taking on the night color of rocks, the pale shimmer of sand. This blessed horse, once more returned to him.

Bin-daa-dee-nin laughed low as the dark shape of the mountain loomed, his heart filled with a prayer to the Mountain Gods.

He had much to be thankful for: a successful raid, with bags filled with food, no loss of life or injury to himself or Yuu-his-kishn, and the return of Moon That Flies. The horse's hooves dug into the rippling sand, tossing it into the air in quick bursts. By tomorrow the wind would have blown sand over those tracks, and Bin-daa-dee-nin would be in the safety of the mountain once again.

The sweet, cooler scent of juniper pine filled his senses as the foothills neared. Bin-daa-dee-nin slowed Moon That Flies to a trot with a tug on his mane as the terrain underfoot shifted from forgiving sand to small, scattered rocks. He did not turn his head at a clatter of hooves behind him but only glanced over when Yuu-his-kishn trotted up beside him. The other Apache rode the long-legged, awkward-looking beast from the ranch, another prize from the raid.

Bin-daa-dee-nin sat back slightly on the horse's back—and was almost thrown as Moon That Flies abruptly stopped dead. Excellent a horseman as he was, Bin-daa-dee-nin barely managed to save himself from a fall by throwing his arms around the horse's neck. Quickly he pushed himself back over the deerskin bag and sat upright again. He was not angry, just puzzled. Why had the horse acted like that?

"Good raid, brother," Yuu-his-kishn said.

"Yes, now you have a horse," Bin-daa-dee-nin replied. "And I have mine back."

Bin-daa-dee-nin still could not believe that his horse had been at that ranch. Although the ranch was not far from the mountain, and the horse would naturally join other animals, he did not expect to see again what was taken from him.

He had lost Moon That Flies in another fierce battle with the soldiers. As Bin-daa-dee-nin led his horse through a narrow crevass in the mountain, a gunshot had almost struck Moon That Flies' head. With a squeal of panic the horse had wrenched the reins from Bin-daa-dee-nin's hand and taken off down the mountainside. Bin-daa-dee-nin had been unable to search for him because he and his brothers had to move their camp immediately. In the following days he had prayed that through the power of the gods, his horse would return to him, but he had not had much hope.

"You are back, my fine horse," he murmured. Now their fortunes would improve.

Moon That Flies had begun to walk forward again, but Bin-daa-dee-nin stopped him by leaning back. Gazing up the black side of the mountain, he felt uneasy. He did not see anything dangerous—and with his perfect eyesight he would have, even though the moonlight had left the mountain—but lately the mountain seemed forbidding, as if it harbored an outswelling of evil spirits. Perhaps the horse would banish those feelings.

Sliding off Moon That Flies, Bin-daa-dee-nin grabbed the horse's mane again. He would have to lead him up the trail to the Apaches' latest camp; even for this surefooted animal the path was too rocky and steep to ride. The horse bumped him affectionately with his nose, tickling Bin-daa-dee-nin's bare shoulder with his whiskers. Bin-daa-dee-nin smiled.

Bin-daa-dee-nin stretched out his senses as he and Moon That Flies climbed the mountain, Yuu-his-kishn following close behind with his horse. The dry, sparse woods shared its secrets of what lay under the blanket of night. That sharp crack of a twig, followed by muffled crunching over pine needles, was a newborn fawn, moving down the mountain with its mother toward morning meadows to feed. The sound of the mother, more cautious, was only a brush of fur against the bristly arms of a four-wing saltbush. Farther away still, the soft, steady plink in a standing pool of water was a black bear drinking.

That was all. Bin-daa-dee-nin shook his head as his thoughts turned inward again and the dark feeling of the mountain rose up against him. He and Yuu-his-kishn had left Nzhų-'a'c-siin sleeping in a small limestone cave near the top of the mountain. Nzhų-'a'c-siin had not recovered from his gunshot wound—he had a scar on his stomach, where the front part of the wound had closed up, but the hole in his back from the bullet had never healed. He still could not ride far without further opening the wound, and although he did not complain, his agony was apparent during even the shortest journey.

More so with every raid, Bin-daa-dee-nin feared to find Nzhų-'a'c-siin gone or dead and the clear signs of soldiers in the camp. *The white eyes are everywhere—stamping through the trees, creeping around my brother's cave,* Bin-daa-dee-nin thought bitterly as he scrambled up a ledge. Moon That Flies hesitated, then bounded up with him in a shower of crumbling rock.

"Wait!" Yuu-his-kishn hissed. "Make sure it's safe."

Bin-daa-dee-nin stopped and forced himself to answer quietly. He and Yuu-his-kishn had argued enough over what to do since they had been living on the mountain. Since Nzhų-'a'c-siin had gotten shot, the arguments had gotten even more frequent and angry. *He cannot see in the night the way I can, and so the terrors of the darkness are great for him,* Bin-daa-dee-nin reminded himself. "I do not see anything," he said at last. "I do not hear or smell anything. The white eyes will not find this camp. We have been here only two days, and they do not search at night."

"You do not have enough respect for them," Yuu-his-kishn snapped. "But you should, because they are many and well armed. We must move the camp."

"No." Bin-daa-dee-nin began to climb the steep hillside again, his fingers brushing fallen pinecones as he searched for rocks to grip. The horse followed him easily now, once again accustomed to his master's ways.

"We'll move when I say," Yuu-his-kishn called, and Bin-daa-dee-nin could tell that the other Apache was standing still on the slope behind him.

Bin-daa-dee-nin stopped, although he longed to reach Nzhų-'a'c-siin. "The white eyes won't search for us over a couple of stolen chickens and a horse—they do not know how to prize animals such as that," he said, pointing at Moon That Flies. Bin-daa-dee-nin did not like arguments, especially ones that could never be settled. But perhaps it was better to have this one now, before they reached Nzhų-'a'c-siin, who might begin to argue also and disturb his wound.

"They might not come for us," Yuu-his-kishn said. Bin-daa-dee-nin saw Moon That Flies nosing the taller horse. The two horses, at least, could agree. "But I do not think we should take the chance of being found," Yuu-his-kishn added.

"But Nzhų-'a'c-siin—" Bin-daa-dee-nin began, his face set in a scowl.

"I know," Yuu-his-kishn interrupted.

"Let us discuss this at first light," Bin-daa-dee-nin said. Without waiting for a response, he gripped Moon That Flies' mane and led him up the deep black of the mountain. The ground had leveled off, and he stepped soundlessly over its pine needle coat. A coyote howled from far away, his wavering voice rising and falling in plaintive song. Bin-daa-dee-nin shivered with distaste. Coyote, the trickster, was bad luck. He only hoped that Coyote's howl wasn't a sign that today's good luck had run out.

He saw the cave where they had left Nzhų-'a'c-siin up ahead, a small hole in a cliff, the darkest of the black night things. Bin-daa-dee-nin crouched by the entrance, his horse crowding behind him. "It's me," he whispered.

He heard a soft shuffling noise, then Nzhų-'a'c-siin's head poked out into the starlight. "Good raid?" he asked.

"Very good." Over his shoulder, Bin-daa-dee-nin saw that Yuu-his-kishn was setting branches together to build a small fire to cook their food. Bin-daa-dee-nin smiled at the thought of good, warm food. The ranchers would not be able to send a message to the army post at Fort Bayard or Fort Cummings until morning. For now, the three Apaches could rest.

Nzhų-'a'c-siin slowly crawled out of the cave. Bin-daa-dee-nin found it difficult to watch his pain. Often when Nzhų-'a'c-siin moved, his wound bled or drained a clear liquid. That couldn't be good, Bin-daa-dee-nin thought, but they could not leave him in the black cave alone all night without food, either.

Nzhų-'a'c-siin leaned against a rock, stretching out his legs in their worn brown boots. He closed his eyes.

Rising, Bin-daa-dee-nin walked over to Moon That Flies, who had joined the tall ranch horse at the edge of the clearing. The deerskin bag on Moon That Flies' back held corn for the horses. "Tomorrow, if there is time, I will take you and this new horse to a meadow to graze," Bin-daa-dee-nin told his horse. He paused, his hands on the bag, thinking. Once the soldiers got the message about the raid, they would clumsily assemble their horses and weapons. Even if they had the help of Apache scouts, the soldiers would not reach the mountains until the sun had begun to sink from its highest point in the sky. Probably the horses could graze for a while first.

Then we must move the camp, Bin-daa-dee-nin thought. He found he agreed with Yuu-his-kishn. Moving would not be good for Nzhų-'a'c-siin, but they had left too many signs here.

Bin-daa-dee-nin opened the bag and removed two dead

chickens. He had seized them so stealthily from the little house on the ranch, the chickens had not even squawked. Bin-daa-dee-nin tossed them to Yuu-his-kishn to clean for the night's meal.

"I can do that," protested Nzhų-'a'c-siin, sitting upright.

Bin-daa-dee-nin glanced over at him. The fire had grown into a living, licking small beast, sharing its light with Nzhų-'a'c-siin. His brother's face was a dusty gray, and his body drooped, broken, against the rock, as if he could not move his arms or legs. Bin-daa-dee-nin's eyes dropped to Nzhų-'a'c-siin's wound. He had wrapped it with a strip of clean, flowered cloth, but the cloth was now stained red, yellow, and crusted brown. Bin-daa-dee-nin wasn't sure, but he thought that more of the strange colors—the yellow and brown—were on the cloth in the past few days. Bin-daa-dee-nin clenched his fist on the bag as an all too familiar feeling overwhelmed him—fear.

That was not right for an Apache warrior to feel. *I must act,* Bin-daa-dee-nin told himself. After they ate, he would rip off a fresh strip of cloth from the big wound-up piece that he had stored in the cave and change Nzhų-'a'c-siin's bandage. Luckily Bin-daa-dee-nin had much of this cloth from a successful raid on the stage. Not long after Nzhų-'a'c-siin had been shot, Bin-daa-dee-nin and Yuu-his-kishn had captured two horses from a small band of Mexican traders and ridden after the stage, whose route and schedule they knew well. From past experience Bin-daa-dee-nin had guessed the stage would have a load of cloth such as this. That had been the main purpose of the raid—to find a bandage and either food or something he could sell for food. He hadn't found much to sell, just a few odd things like a round tin pot that whistled when filled with water over the fire. But perhaps he still didn't know the value of all white people's possessions.

The Mexicans had apparently not taken good care of their

animals, and they had died shortly after the raid, leaving the Apaches without horses once again. Bin-daa-dee-nin had badly missed a horse's help in moving their camp.

Moon That Flies twisted his head back around to look at him, and Bin-daa-dee-nin gave a small smile. The horse was probably wondering when Bin-daa-dee-nin would stop having useless thoughts and feelings and take off the deerskin bag and feed him. Horses were simple like that.

Bin-daa-dee-nin pulled the bag off his back and emptied a measure of corn onto two tin plates for the horses. They began to eat hungrily. Bin-daa-dee-nin looked over his shoulder to see if Yuu-his-kishn had begun to cook their own food and saw the other Apache approaching. "I do not think Nzhų-'a'c-siin will live much longer," he said. "His spirit roams—"

"No talk of death!" Bin-daa-dee-nin snapped. "He lives yet!"

"Barely." Yuu-his-kishn's smooth bronze face gleamed in the firelight, and his black eyes held Bin-daa-dee-nin's own. "Perhaps it is time to take him to the reservation," he said. "You scorn the white eyes' doctors, but sometimes they have good medicine."

"No!" Bin-daa-dee-nin shook his head, busying himself with dividing the last few bits of corn in the bag between the horses. He glared at Yuu-his-kishn.

"I know what you are thinking," Yuu-his-kishn said. "Your mother died on the reservation. And your father too, although not in the same way. That is why you do not want to go, even though we should—"

"Let's eat," Bin-daa-dee-nin said, trying not to hit Yuu-his-kishn in the face for his meddling and bad advice. "The chickens smell good."

Yuu-his-kishn shrugged, then walked to the fire and slid the chickens off the makeshift spit, a stick hung between two towers of stones, onto another tin plate. Nzhų-'a'c-siin watched silently. Yuu-his-kishn ripped the chickens into three parts and handed each of them pieces. Bin-daa-dee-nin tore hungrily into his portion. "Good," he said around a mouthful. The other two Apaches nodded.

"I found some piñon nuts," Nzhų-'a'c-siin offered. He jerked his head toward the cave. "They're in there."

"I'll get them," Bin-daa-dee-nin said, getting to his feet. The sweet, hard nuts were always a treat, but he intended to especially enjoy them since Nzhų-'a'c-siin would have had to crawl painfully for hours to gather them.

He found the nuts in a small deerskin bag. It had a drawstring at the top and had been made by Nzhų-'a'c-siin's sister on the reservation.

The Apaches chewed the nuts without saying anything. Bin-daa-dee-nin didn't want to interrupt his sheer enjoyment with words.

"I'm going to sleep in the cave," Yuu-his-kishn said after they had devoured the last of the nuts. He stood, stretching, and looked at Nzhų-'a'c-siin.

"I'll sleep out here," said Nzhų-'a'c-siin. "In that cave I feel like a bear."

"I will stay with you," said Bin-daa-dee-nin, settling himself cross-legged. He thought Nzhų-'a'c-siin would be too cold out here, since he could move so little, but that was his decision to make. Bin-daa-dee-nin glanced at the two horses, standing close together at the edge of the clearing, and wondered if he should tie them. But they were full of corn now and unlikely to stray from the place where they'd gotten such fine food. Besides, Moon That Flies had never strayed before. He had been stolen and forced to go.

"That is a fine horse," said Nzhų-'a'c-siin, following his gaze.

"Yes. I have never had such an animal," agreed Bin-daa-dee-nin, smiling.

And I do not wish to lose him again, he thought, remembering the battle in which Moon That Flies had gotten away. Bin-daa-dee-nin shook off the memory of this. Tonight was a victory celebration.

When he was a young boy, the Mescalero tribe, including his mother and father, had roamed the mountains, hunting and camping in the traditional way. After a successful hunt or raid, the men would build a huge fire and dance around it, shouting to the sky their victory. They would shower their families with presents.

There will be no such celebration tonight, Bin-daa-dee-nin thought, looking over at Moon That Flies again. The horse stood quietly on three legs, nose to nose with his companion, the starlight a gentle blue glow around him. But Bin-daa-dee-nin was satisfied.

Nzhų-'a'c-siin shifted slowly against the rock. "You are the keen sighted," he said, his voice hoarse. "So, what did you see on your raid?"

"I did not see much—that is why it was a good raid. No fighting." Bin-daa-dee-nin knew that the white eyes thought the Apaches were savage killers, but they did not kill or even fight unless absolutely necessary. They wanted to stay alive themselves, and that meant avoiding trouble. "The white eyes did not come out until we were to the open sands on the horses," he added.

So many small raids are difficult and dangerous, Bin-daa-dee-nin thought. In the old days, the Apaches stole cattle, herded it to Old Mexico, and sold it for food and goods. But the presence of so many soldiers prevented this now, forcing the Apaches to raid frequently for supplies.

Nzhų-'a'c-siin's eyes were closed. He seemed quiet and contented, but that had always been his way.

Bin-daa-dee-nin stared into the curling flames of the fire. He had not killed those ranchers, although he could have slaughtered them in their beds before they even knew he was there. *I let them live, but not because they deserve to.* The ranchers did not belong here, in the way of the dark green junipers and mesquite, twisted and shaped by wind and lack of water, or the jagged gray-and-black cliffs of these mountains, or the broad-leaved mescal plants, with their fleshy, good-tasting roots, that grew on the plains and hills east of here, where he had been born.

He was born on White Mountain, the sacred mountain of the Mescaleros, in the winter, not long after the tribe had fled the reservation. His mother said proudly that she waited to have him on White Mountain so that his life would be blessed. But soon after Bin-daa-dee-nin's birth, the Mescaleros had been forced to return to the reservation. They were starving, and the white agent made promises that they would have food and be safe. Instead the food was too little and rotten, and the agent gave the Mescaleros no protection at all from the savagery of the whites.

Bin-daa-dee-nin kept his eyes on the fire, not wishing to see the swaying of the dark scrub around him or the long shadows cast by the wavering light. Night seemed so like death, where one could not see what was out there, where the sounds were not right for what they came from.

Death does not come silently, he remembered. *Those who are massacred are loud in their pain, as are those who must see such an end to life.*

He had known so much bloody death as a child. One day,

when he was still very young, a group of warriors had left the camp, near the edge of the reservation, to go on a hunt. The women, old men, and children stayed behind, but Bin-daa-dee-nin had sneaked off into the pine forest after the warriors, wanting to see the hunt. He walked to the edge of a cliff and, lying flat on a rough gray outcropping of granite, watched what happened two hundred yards away, in a ravine below.

The hunters were closing in on a deer, moving slowly through the trees, near a small waterfall. And going the other way, white people were creeping through the forest, armed with rifles, headed for the camp. Bin-daa-dee-nin had cried out, but the wind stole the sound.

The whites had butchered all in their path. Yuu-his-kishn had been with the warriors and escaped. Nzhų-'a'c-siin's mother had been shot and scalped, but she had first managed to hide him and his sister under an elk hide. After that he had traveled with Bin-daa-dee-nin's family. Bin-daa-dee-nin's father had been with the warriors at the time of the massacre, and his mother was alone in the forest, gathering berries. They had survived that death, only to meet an even worse one at the hands of the white eyes soon after.

Bin-daa-dee-nin clenched his fists. Sometimes the need for revenge was strong. He remembered that ranch family's screaming. *They are lucky to be alive,* he thought grimly. Still, the ranchers served a purpose. They could be raided, although the next raid on a ranch would not be so easy. The ranchers would be more alert.

The fire had died down to glowing sticks. Bin-daa-dee-nin dropped his head and sighed. He knew in his heart that the ranch raids could not go on forever. A few years ago the ranchers and miners had been just a danger and an offense. But now they could not be avoided. And the army tracked the Apaches all the time. That made hunting for food difficult, so the ranchers and miners had to be raided. Then the army tracked the Apaches with even more men and determination.

Nzhų-'a'c-siin opened his eyes, lifted his head, and smiled. "Do you remember the ambush of the Mexicans?" he asked.

Bin-daa-dee-nin smiled back. "Yes." That had been Victorio's plan. It had really been a grim joke. After the Mescalero warriors had left the reservation with Victorio, they had often gone into Old Mexico to escape the soldiers here. At one time Victorio and his warriors had made a strong camp in the Candelaria Mountains of Mexico, and the Mexicans in a nearby town had discovered their trail. The Mexicans decided to fight the raiding Apaches, but they did not know how many there were or that they had found Victorio's band. A group of Mexicans, mounted on fine horses, had ridden confidently up to the mountains, expecting an easy victory.

But Victorio had prepared an ambush in a deep canyon, littered with huge boulders. Instead of hiding his warriors behind the boulders, he positioned them high on the cliffs, across from the boulders. When the Mexicans rode into the canyon, the Apaches opened fire from across it.

The Mexicans dived for the cover of the boulders. Then the Apaches began firing from behind and above them.

"That was a great battle," said Nzhų-'a'c-siin.

Bin-daa-dee-nin nodded. "We will have others," he promised, and Nzhų-'a'c-siin closed his eyes again.

Bin-daa-dee-nin pushed his face into his hands, his black hair slipping over his fingers. *I must show such cleverness now,* he thought. Moving a wounded man and keeping ahead of the hunters was not easy. But he had no choice. *We cannot go back to the reservation,* he told himself firmly.

That place was like quicksand—so hard to escape, so deadly. He remembered the last time he had seen his mother and father alive. Bin-daa-dee-nin had left Victorio's band just before the snows came and traveled to the reservation. He had been shocked and horrified by what he found. His mother, sick and exhausted, had wasted away into a tall stick of yellow skin and jutting bones. The bright red blood she had coughed seemed the only part of her still alive. His father was dead.

"He was stabbed in a fight," his mother whispered, her breath rattling in her sick lungs. "A fight over nothing, but both men were drunk. A trader sold him bad whiskey. He drank to forget my sickness. . . ."

Bin-daa-dee-nin had fled the reservation, soon after his mother didn't recognize him anymore. A force of sheer anguish, like a stream blocked by logs, had struggled to break through as he ran through many suns and moons, but he did not let it. Instead he had returned to Victorio and the fight to stay free.

Rocking back and forth, Bin-daa-dee-nin gazed at Nzhų-'a'c-siin, feeling baffled and frustrated. With each rise of the sun he was losing. He knew it, but he did not know what to do.

"I think I will rest now." Nzhų-'a'c-siin was already falling into sleep as he spoke.

"Yes." Bin-daa-dee-nin abruptly stood. He wished his brother would not stop talking. *I will bring the horse over to the fire and sleep also,* he decided. The night was still but for the hushed sweep of an owl's wings nearby. Bin-daa-dee-nin listened carefully, but the owl did not return. Already the sun's first gray touch lightened the sky, quieting the animals of the night. *I cannot sleep long—the soldiers will wake with the sun,* he thought. He did not know exactly what to expect from the morning, but he did not want to be caught by surprise. He did know that he would need his horse, and so he should keep Moon That Flies close.

First Bin-daa-dee-nin went to the cave and dug through their small pile of possessions. Most of them he and Yuu-his-kishn had gotten in the stagecoach robbery: two high black hats, a tin cup, the round whistling pot, a pair of brown leather boots, and the flowered cloth. From the bottom of the pile Bin-daa-dee-nin tugged free a brightly colored, fringed Mexican blanket. He brought the heavy, soft blanket back out to the fire, spread it out over Nzhų-'a'c-siin, and tucked the edges tight under him. Good that Nzhų-'a'c-siin was asleep. Although he missed his brother's company, they had talked enough about the old times. Maybe someday they would live with a larger band again, but right now that life no longer existed. They had only what was here. Besides, when Bin-daa-dee-nin thought about the old days with Victorio or the reservation, he thought about the dead, which was forbidden. He had always accepted the teachings of the elders about this, but now he knew why they were right. He had already thought about the dead too much, and now their spirits surrounded him. Sometimes they would not let him go.

He stretched up his arms in the last halo of the night, the wind cold between his fingers. "Guide me," he whispered, letting his spirit rise to the sky that he saw so clearly. Surely the Mountain Gods lived here, in the massive gray rocks of this high, strong place. "Tell me what I must do."

Moon That Flies whickered quietly, and Bin-daa-dee-nin glanced at him. The horse was barely visible in the last weak orange light of the fire. Bin-daa-dee-nin dropped his arms. He must plan for tomorrow. He would let the fire burn out and, at first light, completely hide any sign of it and his and Yuu-his-kishn's tracks through the woods.

Bin-daa-dee-nin walked over to the horse, his hand out, reaching for him. "Come," he said. Moon That Flies followed him willingly to the fire, understanding what he wanted. Bin-daa-dee-nin sat back on the sandy ground, dropping his head onto his knees. The horse touched him with his nose, and Bin-daa-dee-nin reached up, encircling Moon That Flies' warm neck with his arms, breathing in the sweaty, earthy, good scent of the animal. It was not an Apache warrior's way, but whether Moon That Flies had power or not, he was no ordinary horse. Bin-daa-dee-nin wrapped his arms around his legs and closed his eyes. He had much to do. But now he would sleep, listening to the soft breaths of his horse and brother, close to him around the fire, alive and magic, a gift from the gods.

Perhaps he had not lost all.

9

Bin-daa-dee-nin dropped the jackrabbit he had just caught onto a smooth slab of rock and sat down beside it, reaching for his knife to clean it. The clear eye of the sun gleamed high overhead, destroying the shadows and putting the birds to sleep. Bin-daa-dee-nin tipped back his head, the thick scent of sun-warmed sage and soft hum of insects close to him, until he felt as one with the day.

Footsteps approached, and Bin-daa-dee-nin turned to see Nzhų-'a'c-siin.

"You had luck on your hunt," Nzhų-'a'c-siin said, looking down at him. Over the past few moons, as the sun had gotten stronger, so had Nzhų-'a'c-siin. He could now walk, although riding was still difficult. He had recovered since the Apaches had not had to move camp so much—the soldiers had been quiet for a while. That happened sometimes, Bin-daa-dee-nin knew. Perhaps they had other duties besides tracking Apaches.

"Yes, we will eat well tonight," Bin-daa-dee-nin replied, touching the jackrabbit's soft, gray-brown fur. *More than we have been,* he thought.

Moon That Flies shook himself, scattering flies, then began to graze the sparse tufts of grass that grew between the rocks and trees. He was thin too but seemed able to survive on the scanty grass. The other horse from the ranch also had adapted to life with the Apaches. But the two animals had to search for food all day and night.

Yuu-his-kishn approached around a large rock. Bin-daa-dee-nin noticed that his hands were empty—he had not succeeded in his hunt. "Good, you found something," Yuu-his-kishn said, sitting next to Bin-daa-dee-nin on the sandy dirt. "But that rabbit is not much for three."

"We've got to go on a big raid again," Bin-daa-dee-nin said. Yuu-his-kishn had not wanted to raid for a long time because of the danger, but maybe he was hungry enough now to agree to it. "We're out of ammunition, and we don't have any more food."

Yuu-his-kishn frowned. "The soldiers have not been chasing us because we have not raided," he said.

"They may have gone elsewhere." Bin-daa-dee-nin picked up his knife and examined the rabbit. "Surely they do not only track us."

"Yes, they do," Yuu-his-kishn snapped. "That is why the fort is there, at the foot of the mountain—so that the soldiers can kill Apaches attacking the stage."

"We should go back to Mexico to escape them, then," Bin-daa-dee-nin said, his own voice sharpening. "That must be our plan before snow falls."

"I will be able to ride soon," Nzhų-'a'c-siin said, sitting beside the other two boys.

"Mexico is where Victorio was killed!" Yuu-his-kishn ground his teeth. "And now the Mexican army is working with the American soldiers to kill Apaches."

"We must get you a horse," Bin-daa-dee-nin said to Nzhų-'a'c-siin, ignoring Yuu-his-kishn. He walked over to Moon That Flies, and the pinto raised his head and whickered, as he always did. Bin-daa-dee-nin stroked his sleek neck. Moon That Flies had not had much corn to eat, the way he probably had on that ranch, but he still seemed in good health. *I would like to get you good food,* Bin-daa-dee-nin thought. He wanted to raid for all of them and celebrate with a feast.

"After we get another horse, we will ride to the reservation," Yuu-his-kishn said from behind him.

"I will not surrender to white eyes with guns!" Bin-daa-dee-nin whipped around to face the other Apache. "Death would be swift!"

"So you wish us to be shot like rabbits as we run across the mountain?" Yuu-his-kishn stared at him, his expression equally furious.

Bin-daa-dee-nin kept silent until he could control his words. Victorio had never shouted at the warriors in his band. "We must scout," he said finally. "To plan a raid so that we can get Nzhų-'a'c-siin a horse. We can do nothing until we accomplish that."

"Very well." Yuu-his-kishn lifted his horse's bridle from a tree branch.

"What do you think we should do?" Bin-daa-dee-nin asked Nzhų-'a'c-siin. Before, Nzhų-'a'c-siin had not wanted to return to the reservation. If the two of them still agreed, perhaps they could yet persuade Yuu-his-kishn.

"Find a horse," Nzhų-'a'c-siin said, looking up at him. His color was better, although his cheeks were still sunken. "I do not know if I can ride as far as Mexico or the reservation now. But I will keep getting better."

Bin-daa-dee-nin nodded. He still did not think Nzhų-'a'c-siin could survive on the reservation. Nzhų-'a'c-siin's wound did not spill so much fluid as it had at first, but it had still not closed up completely in his back. Bin-daa-dee-nin did not know if it ever would.

"Let us go," Yuu-his-kishn said, swinging easily onto his tall horse's back. He had no saddle, but since they had no more ammunition for the guns, they would not have to carry them awkwardly in their hands.

"I will prepare the rabbit while you are gone," Nzhų-'a'c-siin said, and Bin-daa-dee-nin was grateful for his calm, steady voice.

Bin-daa-dee-nin walked over to Moon That Flies, who tossed his head eagerly. Perhaps he, too, was ready to get away from this mountain and search for better food. Bin-daa-dee-nin easily jumped onto his back, sliding forward into place. For luck Bin-daa-dee-nin turned the pinto south. That direction had the Mescalero feeling of green and had always been Bin-daa-dee-nin's favorite way to go. Despite the danger, Bin-daa-dee-nin looked forward to a raid. He did not like to sit in camp and weigh one side of a question, then the other. *Soon Nzhų-'a'c-siin will be able to travel far,* he told himself, leaning back to brace himself as Moon That Flies picked his way down the rocky mountainside. *Then we will be free.*

At the bottom of the mountain Bin-daa-dee-nin looked out over the desert. The large sun, burning with its summer strength, dispelled the shadows. The desert was flat and quiet, and no clouds of soldiers' dust spoiled the air. Bin-daa-dee-nin let the reins fall through his hands and nudged Moon That Flies with his heels. That was the signal for the horse to run, but the pinto hesitated, rolling his large brown eyes back to look at Bin-daa-dee-nin. He had stopped in this way ever since Bin-daa-dee-nin had taken him from that ranch. Obviously the ranchers had taught him to hold back his speed so that they could use him for work. "Out here, a horse must run," Bin-daa-dee-nin said. "Remember?"

Bin-daa-dee-nin touched up the horse again with his heels. He had pushed harder with one heel than the other, and Moon That Flies sidestepped. Looking down, Bin-daa-dee-nin saw that in this unusual manner of walking, the horse was actually crossing his legs over each other. *Why would the ranchers teach a horse this strange trick?* he wondered. Bin-daa-dee-nin firmly squeezed his legs against his horse's sides, and Moon That Flies broke into a choppy trot, then a slow gallop. "Better," Bin-daa-dee-nin told him, leaning forward. "But go very fast now, like the wind of a storm."

Suddenly the pinto threw up his head and burst into a dead-out run, his slender white legs a blur against the sand. Bin-daa-dee-nin gripped Moon That Flies lightly with his legs, easily taking into his own body the jarring of the horse's strides, melding their movements into one. Bin-daa-dee-nin let out a soft whoop and pressed his cheek against Moon That Flies' neck as they raced south. "Now you are my horse," he whispered.

Behind him he heard the pounding hooves of Yuu-his-kishn's horse. Yuu-his-kishn had trained his clumsy beast from the ranch to stretch out his legs. "Where are we going?" he yelled.

"The other ranch!" Bin-daa-dee-nin turned Moon That Flies slightly, pointing him at the second ranch he had seen only from the mountain. He noticed that the horse was much easier to turn than he had been before his capture, even when he ran fast.

Yuu-his-kishn caught up on his long-legged horse, galloping beside them. He grinned, his teeth white in his dark face, and Bin-daa-dee-nin smiled back. The two Apaches swiftly, tirelessly crossed the desert on their horses, the soft thunder of hooves on sand the only sound.

At the bottom of a small rise, Bin-daa-dee-nin pulled Moon That Flies to a halt. Yuu-his-kishn stopped his horse just behind them. The horses were excited from their run, and Bin-daa-dee-nin waited until they had stopped prancing and blowing before walking Moon That Flies slowly uphill until he could just see the ranch over the lift of ground.

The breeze blew Bin-daa-dee-nin's black hair, and he pushed it behind his shoulders so that he could see clearly. Before him were a large adobe house and tin-roofed barn. Next to them was a corral with two mules inside. Mules were of little use: they could carry heavy packs, but they couldn't run.

Mules are good to eat, but we cannot capture one for that, Bin-daa-dee-nin thought. This ranch seemed much like the other one. Probably they could not get much food from a quick run through the house, and it would be dangerous. These ranchers would certainly be on the alert after the Apaches' raid on the other ranch.

Carefully he and Yuu-his-kishn backed their horses down the rise. "It's not good," Bin-daa-dee-nin said when they were completely hidden again.

"I agree," said Yuu-his-kishn, wiping sweat from his forehead with his sleeve. "What about raiding miners again? They have much food since they go many days on the trail."

Bin-daa-dee-nin frowned. "They will kill us." Although a few days of scouting would almost certainly reveal another mule train of miners with their silver, heading down the mountain, he didn't want to face those peculiar white men again. They would really rather die than let go of their treasure. "We could attack the stage again," he said. "But we did not get much of value the last time. And the stagecoach drivers are heavily armed."

"Everyone will kill us," Yuu-his-kishn replied, leaning back on his bony horse. "We could raid Silver City."

"How?" Bin-daa-dee-nin asked in surprise. He knew that Silver City was a big gathering of white people and where the miners took their silver. But white people in large numbers were what they were trying to avoid. "Why not just raid wagons going there?" For a time, Victorio's band often raided the wagons headed for Silver City.

"We need food and ammunition now," Yuu-his-kishn said.

"Those wagons are mostly full of useless silver. But the stores in Silver City have what we need, all piled up and ready to take."

"That place is full of white men! We will be shot a thousand times." Bin-daa-dee-nin shook his head. It was not like Yuu-his-kishn to come up with so bold a plan. *Even he should be afraid of so many white people!* Bin-daa-dee-nin thought. *I do not want to hear more of this.* Without another word, Bin-daa-dee-nin turned Moon That Flies to head back to the mountain.

Yuu-his-kishn reached over and grabbed his arm. "We will not be shot in the city if we are fast. People who sell flour are not as quick to reach for a gun as miners. What other choice do we have?"

None, Bin-daa-dee-nin realized. They were returning to Nzhų-'a'c-siin empty-handed, and the hunting was poor on the mountain. "If we get enough supplies from Silver City, we can head for Mexico," he said. "At least then our risk of death will have some purpose."

"After this great raid, we will have supplies to travel wherever we decide to go." Yuu-his-kishn shrugged. "We cannot stay on the mountain much longer."

Bin-daa-dee-nin nodded. "A raid on Silver City will bring many soldiers."

"I do not know why you want to go to Mexico," Yuu-his-kishn said. "Soldiers will be watching the border. And the Mexican soldiers will want to kill us too, once we are in Mexico."

"Yes, but they aren't good soldiers," Bin-daa-dee-nin answered. "Our chances of escaping them are better."

Moon That Flies began to walk back toward camp. In a moment Bin-daa-dee-nin heard Yuu-his-kishn's horse trotting after them, then the hoofbeats stopped. "Let us scout the city," he called.

Bin-daa-dee-nin shook his head vigorously without looking around.

"Stop," Yuu-his-kishn demanded.

Bin-daa-dee-nin slowly pulled Moon That Flies to a halt. Then he turned to face Yuu-his-kishn. "We cannot get close to that place to scout," he said. "So many white eyes go in and out—we will be seen. Our raid will succeed only if we have surprise. That is our one advantage. That and the night."

"We'll raid in daylight," Yuu-his-kishn said.

Bin-daa-dee-nin stared at the other Apache in disbelief. "No! We'll be shot full of holes when they see us."

Moon That Flies skittered sideways. He could tell that his rider was upset. Bin-daa-dee-nin knew that horses were sensitive that way.

"The people in Silver City will be afraid when they see us," Yuu-his-kishn said, looking to the southwest. From riding with Victorio, Bin-daa-dee-nin knew that was where Silver City was, although he had never actually seen the great gathering of white people. "Everyone will run inside," Yuu-his-kishn continued. "We have to go in the light or we won't be able to see what we're getting out of the stores. Even with the light of a full moon, the inside of the stores will be dark."

"We could take torches." Bin-daa-dee-nin simply could not imagine all of those white eyes on him as he stole from their stores. He had once feared the night, a time of ghosts and shadows, but he had become used to the time of dark and moon, even the owls. They were the discontented dead returned, but even what they would do was more predictable than what would happen on a daylight raid.

"But we'd have to break into the buildings at night, and the noise would summon men with guns," Yuu-his-kishn said. "Then we would be the ones surprised. We will raid when the sun is highest. No one will expect a raid then, because they do not think horses can survive a long ride under the eye of the summer sun."

"Your horse may not survive," Bin-daa-dee-nin said. He was more confident that Moon That Flies wouldn't let him down.

"He has stayed alive this long. But perhaps I can find a better one in Silver City." Yuu-his-kishn glanced at the sun. "We can do this now. I know of a hole with water not far from the city. We can go there, then on our raid." The other Apache kicked his horse and galloped toward the southwest and the city that could not be seen.

Bin-daa-dee-nin touched up Moon That Flies with his heels and followed. The black-and-white horse gleamed in the hot light, and his ears flicked back as he awaited new commands from his rider. *I hope my brother is right to do this raid,* Bin-daa-dee-nin thought as the horses sped across the land. *Or we will die in our own blood. Death will be very swift.*

"There's the general store," Yuu-his-kishn said, carefully sticking his head around a tree just outside Silver City. The two Apaches and their horses were behind a small grove of trees, barely tall enough to hide them. "That's where we'll find food and ammunition."

Bin-daa-dee-nin peered at the utter confusion of the town ahead. Moon That Flies pricked his ears as a swinging door banged against a wood wall, and Bin-daa-dee-nin gripped his reins tightly. He hoped the horse wouldn't be too frightened of the strange noises and sights once they entered the town.

"That is a saloon," said Yuu-his-kishn as two cowboys staggered out the door that had just opened, clutching each other for balance. One of the cowboy's hats fell off, and he groped on the dirt street, trying to retrieve it. "The town has many such places."

"All full of ranchers and miners with guns," Bin-daa-dee-nin said. He could see clearly that the two cowboys wore belts with pistols. Both cowboys bent over and together picked up the hat. Then they lurched to their horses, tied to one of the many rails in front of the buildings, and rode down the street, out of the town.

"We will have to be swift," Yuu-his-kishn admitted.

"How do you know that is the store?" Bin-daa-dee-nin asked. All the buildings looked the same to him: made of wood or brick, with tall windows of glass. The smooth, dusty dirt street ran between them.

"I can read the sign. Besides, the agent told me at the reservation."

A stagecoach piled high with goods rattled into town, pulled by a team of eight mules. *We could quickly take what we wanted from that stage,* Bin-daa-dee-nin thought. But that would not be the kind of raid to get them enough food for Mexico.

Three men in vests stood in front of one of the buildings, talking. "Let us wait until they go inside the bank," Yuu-his-kishn said. "Then we strike."

"Why wait only for them?" Bin-daa-dee-nin asked. "So many are outside."

"They look like leaders," Yuu-his-kishn replied. "The bank is where the money is. I think those men will be quick to shoot."

Bin-daa-dee-nin had seen crowds before, on the reservation, but the ragged, sick people were nothing like these. He watched the people in the town carefully, trying to tell them apart. Although at first they had seemed to be walking in all directions, he saw now that most of them were headed for somewhere. Women, wearing long clothes that covered them so completely, he could not see their feet, floated along like strange flowers sailing across a stream. Some of the women went into the building called the bank, some into other buildings, but not the saloons, and a few into the general store.

Good that they are in the store, Bin-daa-dee-nin thought. *Perhaps the men will not shoot when women are in the way.*

A team of well-fed horses pulling a buckboard trotted down the broad dirt street and stopped in front of one of the saloons. The drivers hopped down and began unloading big wood barrels, hooped with metal. Bin-daa-dee-nin's eyes widened greedily as he saw a man in a cowboy hat tie a fine, glossy chestnut loosely to the rail in front of the general store.

The men in vests laughed, and one slapped another on the back. Then they went into the bank.

"Now we go," said Yuu-his-kishn, stepping back to his horse. "We will run the horses straight to the store."

"Then what?" Bin-daa-dee-nin asked. He could feel his senses coming alert as the time came for this most daring of raids. The sky snapped into clarity, the three long white clouds stretching across it sharp edged against the wide turquoise blue. The sigh of the trees bending in the wind became the clicking and swaying of many individual branches, and the clutter of noise from the city changed into voices: the deep tones of the men, the rapid exchanges of the women, and the high-pitched cry of a child from a strange little wheeled carrier. "We cannot leave the horses while we are in the store," Bin-daa-dee-nin said firmly.

"We will have to, for a short time." Yuu-his-kishn picked up his horse's reins. "We can tie them to the hitching rail outside the store."

"They will be stolen!" Bin-daa-dee-nin could not bear to think of Moon That Flies alone in the town, with all those white hands reaching out for him.

"That is why we must be quick!" Yuu-his-kishn was getting angry again. His horse, sensing his rider's strong feelings, was trying to plunge ahead.

Quickly Bin-daa-dee-nin shut out his angry and frightened

thoughts. He must see, hear, and move fast now.

In one bold leap the Apaches burst from the trees on their horses and raced down the wide street at a gallop. Bin-daa-dee-nin's breath whistled in his ears, and he could feel his heart pounding in his chest. *Strange—no one seems to see us,* he thought. They were almost to the general store.

"*Injuns!*" somebody screamed. Bin-daa-dee-nin jerked his head around and saw a whiskery old man, clutching a huge brown bottle, standing outside one of the saloons. The man backed away through the swinging doors into the saloon, his face contorted in terror.

Someone else screamed, and Yuu-his-kishn's horse reared. He slid off to the side, flung the horse's reins around the hitching rail, and ran into the store.

I will not leave you, my horse, Bin-daa-dee-nin thought grimly. Now the whole town seemed to be screaming all around him. He dug his heels into Moon That Flies' sides, urging him up the two wood steps. If the horse reared or refused, Bin-daa-dee-nin knew he would lose most of his time to raid and perhaps be shot. But his horse clattered right up the steps. Bin-daa-dee-nin saw Yuu-his-kishn's eyes widen, then the other Apache swung open the store doors so that horse and rider could pass inside. Moon That Flies pounded across the wood floorboards as if he had been in buildings all his life.

Three white people inside the store stared at them, jaws dropping. A short man with no hair, wearing a white apron, stood behind the long dark wood counter.

"*Ay-eeeee!*" yelled Yuu-his-kishn.

The hairless man's face moved, but he said nothing. Then he ran out the back door. The two other white people, a woman and a man in a vest, backed slowly toward the door as well. The woman was waving her arms and saying something, but the two Apaches ignored her.

"The hairless one will get a gun," said Yuu-his-kishn, grabbing a stack of white socks from the nearest shelf. "We have little time now."

Bin-daa-dee-nin looked quickly around the store. It had shelves and shelves of goods, stretching almost to the high ceiling. The reservation store looked something like this, only here the shelves held enormous piles of food and goods instead of bare spaces. *Do not stand and stare,* Bin-daa-dee-nin ordered himself, sliding off Moon That Flies' back. Yuu-his-kishn was sweeping sacks of food with writing on them into his deerskin bag. Since he could read, he could take what they needed: they hoped to get coffee, sugar, salt, and bacon on this raid. Bin-daa-dee-nin glanced across the shelves, looking for the ammunition. Boxes of it were stacked next to a row of guns. Bin-daa-dee-nin opened his own deerskin bag and pushed in the entire contents of the shelf. He could feel Moon That Flies nosing his back.

"Let's go!" Yuu-his-kishn shouted, running to the door.

Throwing the heavy bag over his shoulder, Bin-daa-dee-nin raced to one of the lowest shelves and seized a pile of checked flannel shirts. The sun was hot and bright now, but soon the nights would be cool, and he would not have another chance to raid Silver City. Bin-daa-dee-nin stuffed the shirts into his bag and leapt onto his horse's back, balancing the full sack in front of him.

Bin-daa-dee-nin hesitated, looking at the long counter. The front was glass, and behind it he could see containers full of brightly colored and striped candy. Quickly he pressed his heel into his horse's side. Moon That Flies sidestepped to the counter, and Bin-daa-dee-nin leaned over and grabbed many sticks of hard candy from behind the glass. He dropped the candy in the sack, then reached for another handful.

A shot rang out in the street. Bin-daa-dee-nin wheeled his horse and trotted him out the door, then he and Moon That Flies plunged down the steps. Fewer people were on the streets than before, and many of the windows of the buildings were closed up. The chestnut was still tied to the rail, abandoned by his owner.

Yuu-his-kishn motioned frantically from down the street.

A horse for Nzhų-'a'c-siin! Bin-daa-dee-nin thought. He pulled his own horse's head around and grabbed the chestnut's reins, releasing him from the hitching rail. Glancing behind him, he saw a crowd of armed men racing toward him, shouting.

"*Hi-yah!*" Bin-daa-dee-nin yelled, and dug his heels into his horse's sides. Moon That Flies leapt forward, dragging the chestnut. A shot whistled by the chestnut's head, and the frightened animal plunged forward. The jerk almost unseated Bin-daa-dee-nin, and he fought to hang on to the new horse and keep the bag of goods from slipping to the ground. Luckily Moon That Flies knew what to do and raced after Yuu-his-kishn without guidance.

At the edge of town Yuu-his-kishn yanked his galloping horse's head west, turning him away from the mountain. *So I will go the other way,* Bin-daa-dee-nin thought, pointing Moon That Flies toward the black of east. Bin-daa-dee-nin had the heavier load and was pulling the new horse as well, and so Yuu-his-kishn had given him the shorter way back. *The white eyes must now go two ways in their hunt,* Bin-daa-dee-nin thought. That would better the chances that one of the Apaches, at least, would return to the mountain.

10

Sharp edges of moon, dark light of night, Bin-daa-dee-nin thought, loosening the reins to let Moon That Flies have his head as they picked their way down the mountain for the last time. By the glow of the full moon, the three Apaches were riding to Mexico. Two moons had passed since the raid on Silver City, and the angry soldiers had been grim and determined in their pursuit. The mountain had been thick with their shouts and gunshots.

Nzhų-'a'c-siin's horse stumbled, and Bin-daa-dee-nin looked quickly back. "Steady, brown one," Nzhų-'a'c-siin murmured, touching his horse's neck. "We have far to go."

"You are all right?" Bin-daa-dee-nin couldn't help asking. Nzhų-'a'c-siin had recovered much from his wound, but he had only ridden his horse around the camp. They had wanted to save Nzhų-'a'c-siin's strength for this long ride.

"Good." Nzhų-'a'c-siin smiled. "I like moving again."

Bin-daa-dee-nin tossed him two sticks of the hard candy from Silver City. Nzhų-'a'c-siin caught them in his free hand, then handed one of the sticks to Yuu-his-kishn, who had drawn up beside him on this broader part of an old elk trail. Bin-daa-dee-nin slowly ate the candy, savoring the sweet, tangy taste. "You have my horse to thank for this sweet," he told the others.

Yuu-his-kishn snorted. "You are strange about that horse," he said. "He is not a person or a god."

"But he is very good for raids," Bin-daa-dee-nin replied. He had never told his brothers about the dream he'd had before Moon That Flies appeared, when the Mountain Gods danced in the cave. *That was the night Nzhų-'a'c-siin was shot,* he remembered. *He could not listen to what I had to say then. And I do not think that Yuu-his-kishn believes in the Mountain Gods anymore.*

Bin-daa-dee-nin bent over the horse's neck, breathing in his warm, dusky, familiar scent. "I do not wish to be without you," he whispered, hoping that the sharp ears of the other Apaches did not catch his words.

His horse flicked an ear, listening. Bin-daa-dee-nin smiled, leaning back to enjoy the steady rhythm of Moon That Flies' swaying strides. Bin-daa-dee-nin had found some good grass on the back side of the mountain, and for almost a moon he had taken the three horses there almost every day to graze. Although the horses were not fat and round like the white people's animals, their coats had become shiny and pleasing in the sun, and their ribs had disappeared under muscle.

"Soon we will have other good things to eat in Mexico," Bin-daa-dee-nin said to his brothers.

"Fine fruits," Nzhų-'a'c-siin agreed. "Yellow bananas and juicy oranges."

"Do not forget coconuts," Yuu-his-kishn said, adjusting his tall black hat.

"And the big birds that talk," Nzhų-'a'c-siin said. "I will have one for a pet to ride on my shoulder."

"You have become as strange about animals as Bin-daa-dee-nin," Yuu-his-kishn said scornfully.

"High in the mountains of Mexico, we will be safe," Bin-daa-dee-nin said, ignoring Yuu-his-kishn's last words.

"And warm," Nzhų-'a'c-siin said.

"Not if we're in the high mountains," Yuu-his-kishn said. "Only there can we avoid the soldiers."

And even Victorio was killed in the mountains of Mexico, Bin-daa-dee-nin could not help thinking. Although the sun burned hot in the dark blue afternoon sky, for a moment he felt cold and uneasy.

"The soldiers may not pursue us since we are few and will not raid much," Nzhų-'a'c-siin said. "We may be able to live like before, when the band of our families was together. I think about those days often. Do you remember when our families found the mescal plants and made good food?"

Bin-daa-dee-nin looked over his shoulder again. "And we did not have candy, but we had the sweet prickly pear fruits," he said.

"It has been many years since our families could gather mescal and prickly pear." Yuu-his-kishn shook his head. "You should not think so much about the old days."

"Those who come after us must know our story," Nzhų-'a'c-siin said wistfully.

Nzhų-'a'c-siin is brave to remember those days, Bin-daa-dee-nin thought. It was hard to think of what had been lost. "Do you think others will come after us?" he asked. "We are hunted, and death haunts the reservation."

"Others will come," Yuu-his-kishn said. "Some of us will survive—perhaps we all will."

Bin-daa-dee-nin glanced back at Yuu-his-kishn, but his brother's face revealed nothing. Bin-daa-dee-nin hid his own surprise. "I did not think you believed we would live to reach Mexico," he said.

Yuu-his-kishn was silent for a long time. "I also hope for this," he said at last.

Bin-daa-dee-nin dug in his deerskin bag for the last strips of meat from a jackrabbit. *Perhaps it is right to hope,* he thought. He turned again on his horse to invite his brothers to share the meat.

A flash of light exploded over his head and smashed into a nearby tree. Moon That Flies shied, and Bin-daa-dee-nin grabbed his mane, barely managing to stay on.

"A howitzer!" Yuu-his-kishn screamed. "Run!"

The word meant nothing to Bin-daa-dee-nin, but the great bringer of death fired again, knocking over another tree and setting the grass on fire. Smoke billowed out, burying him and Moon That Flies in thick, choking gray. Bin-daa-dee-nin gasped, pulling his horse's head away from the fires. A bullet zinged by his head and ricocheted off a rock, whining as it flew into the sand.

The bullets meant the soldiers were close. Bin-daa-dee-nin could no longer see Nzhų-'a'c-siin and Yuu-his-kishn.

Bin-daa-dee-nin turned Moon That Flies toward the south, wishing for a sign of green to appear through the heavy gray smoke. *Mexico,* he thought. *We've got to reach Mexico.* . . . The smoke cleared for an instant and he saw the soldiers climbing the mountainside. *Never have I seen so many,* he realized. They were like red ants, crawling everywhere, ready to sting.

Moon That Flies bounced up and down on his front feet, ready to panic. *The battle frightens him,* Bin-daa-dee-nin thought. *But I cannot stop now to calm him.* Bin-daa-dee-nin urged the horse forward with his heels but was forced almost immediately to pull him around to avoid a line of soldiers. The fire burned brightly in front of them, the heat scorching his skin. Moon That Flies shook his head and snorted, then plunged away from the fire and soldiers. "That is the right thing to do," Bin-daa-dee-nin said, hoping his voice would calm the frightened horse. Then he realized they were headed for a canyon with no way out.

If I could find my brothers, we could climb the sides of the canyon and ambush the soldiers, he thought. The smoke abruptly lifted again, and he saw Yuu-his-kishn up on top of one side of the canyon. A flying bullet shot off Yuu-his-kishn's hat, and he galloped his horse away, back up the mountain. *Good that he got away—and we are too few for an ambush,* Bin-daa-dee-nin realized. Glancing behind him, he saw that the soldiers were coming closer, fanning out from their lines, and the bullets were hitting rocks and the sand like raindrops. *I cannot use cleverness here, with so many attacking,* Bin-daa-dee-nin thought, willing away despair.

The smooth rock face at the end of the canyon rose before him, climbing into the sky. Bin-daa-dee-nin forced Moon That Flies around to face the soldiers. The men were so close, he could see the yellow, brown, and red of their beards and the gleaming gold buttons on their blue uniforms.

Moon That Flies trembled under him. Bin-daa-dee-nin gripped his rifle, but he did not dare raise it. *They will kill me, but also my horse,* he thought. *They would not mean to shoot a useful animal, but the soldiers cannot shoot well. I cannot let this horse die. I must surrender.*

A howling filled the earth and sky as the great weapon called a howitzer fired again. Terrified, Moon That Flies reared with a loud whinny. Bin-daa-dee-nin grabbed his mane but found himself looking directly into the blue eyes of a soldier—with the butt of his rifle raised. A heavy blow hit Bin-daa-dee-nin's shoulders, and he fell off his horse onto the rocks and dirt. Thick smoke from the howitzer blew across the canyon, climbing its walls and dropping back down to the sand. Bin-daa-dee-nin pushed himself up quickly with his hands and looked frantically around for his horse, but he could see nothing in the gray clouds.

Before the blast, he had seen that one wall of the cliff was pocked with holes. An Apache could climb it, although not a horse. The soldiers were firing into the smoke, trying to hit him by chance. But the shots were hitting below the cliff—the soldiers did not expect him to climb.

I must live! Bin-daa-dee-nin told himself. *If I see other days, perhaps I can find my horse and my brothers.*

The climb up the cliff face was difficult, and he had to remind himself to place each hand and foot carefully on the rough, crumbling surface and not fall back into the battle. At the top of the canyon, free of the smoke and gunfire, Bin-daa-dee-nin heaved himself over the rim and began to run back up the mountain. He did not stop until he was sure none of the bullets could reach him.

He blinked, trying to clear the sting of the smoke from his eyes. Below, he could see the fires, slowly dying, and the soldiers scattering across the mountain. Nzhų-'a'c-siin and Yuu-his-kishn did not seem to be prisoners, but he could not see all that was happening. "No scouts are with the army," Bin-daa-dee-nin whispered. "I will not be followed so high."

Bin-daa-dee-nin searched across the battlefield for his horse, but he did not see Moon That Flies' black-and-white coat. Bin-daa-dee-nin had been in enough battles to know that his horse probably lived, despite the soldiers' bad shooting. Yuu-his-kishn and Nzhų-'a'c-siin had also probably not been shot or perhaps had gotten away. Except for Nzhų-'a'c-siin's one time of bad luck, they had always escaped. But Bin-daa-dee-nin could not help thinking that this time perhaps his brothers had not.

A feeling of loneliness gripped him, so terrible that he dropped to his knees. *Am I the only one alive?* he wondered. *Have the gods taken my horse and left me?*

He looked up at the sky. It had lost the sun behind the mountain and had no answer.

Part IV

DEATH ON THE MOUNTAIN

11

I'm so worried about *Mama* and *Zachary,* Sarah wrote in her diary. *They are still very weak. But I know it is a miracle that both have survived this long.*

She looked over at her mother, who sat across from her in the living room, mending a sock. The lamplight shone on Mama's thin, lovely face. Rachel had already gone to bed, and Zachary slept in the wood cradle that Papa had made for him. Sarah tapped her pen against the page, then looked out the small window, framing a square of the night.

> *I find it difficult to concentrate since the events of four months ago, when Moon Dancer was stolen and Zachary born. Although my family is safe, I feel I cannot take that for granted one minute. Papa is now out in the barn, retrieving a harness to oil, and my heart is pounding from fear for him. What if something befalls him? I know it is unlikely that the Apaches will come back—they took what they wanted, and, as Papa says, they have likely moved on or been killed. But we do not know.*
>
> *I myself have been unable to move on. Papa and Mama*

have asked me several times if I want another horse. Hearing by telegraph of my plight, Grandma Chilton offered to send me a splendid horse from Fort Smith. That was very kind of her, but I simply do not want to replace my horse. I did enjoy a rare smile, imagining the first impressions of a fine horse from Fort Smith of this wild country.

My fear has made me lonely even when I am in the midst of my family, because I do not really feel that they are mine to keep. I know that I must resolve this and be strong, but I have not found a way. I brood too much over the loss of my horse, this is certain, but it is hard to think of other matters—

Sarah's head jerked up as the door swung open with a loud creak. Papa walked in, carrying the black leather harness, his boots squeaking on the floorboards. Sarah felt her shoulders slump with relief.

"Come into the kitchen for your lessons," Mama said to Sarah, setting her sewing aside. "It's high time we started them again."

"Mama, I don't need lessons—just rest yourself," Sarah said quickly. "You should go to bed."

"Yes, you need your lessons." Mama's voice was firm. She rose from the rocking chair, gripping the arm for support. "Just because we live on the frontier doesn't mean you can grow up ignorant."

Papa tilted his head toward Sarah and frowned. Sarah knew what that look meant: Don't aggravate your mama.

"Let's go in the kitchen," Mama said. "The light is better."

Zachary made a soft noise in his cradle. Sarah put her pen in the inkwell, then crossed the room to her brother. Zachary lay on his back in the cradle, raising his small arms. "Sweet boy," Sarah cooed, putting out a finger for him to grip. Zachary's bright blue eyes were fixed on her face. Just this week he had started smiling. *He is not a plump cherub like the Hanleys' baby girl, although they are about the same age,* Sarah thought, remembering the granddaughter of the stage stop's owners. *But perhaps he doesn't have to be?*

"Come, Sarah," Mama called from the kitchen.

"I must go learn," Sarah said to the baby, gently withdrawing her finger. Zachary let her go with a whimper of protest. *If I were Rachel and left him, he would full-out yell,* Sarah thought. Rachel and Zachary—or Zach, as she called him—had a special bond. Rachel was so young herself, she seemed able to enter Zachary's baby world in a way the older people could not. They spoke their own language together.

Sarah took her place at the kitchen table and opened her history book, which Mama had made sure to bring from Fort Smith. "We must pray for President McKinley," Mama said, closing her eyes.

"Why?" Sarah asked, propping her chin in her hand.

"Because he lies near death," Mama said sternly. "A lunatic shot him this July."

"Oh," Sarah said. She felt her eyes drawn to the kitchen window and through it into the vast, empty night. "So what happens if President McKinley dies?" she asked, forcing herself to listen to what Mama was saying.

"*Sarah,*" Mama reproved her. "This is not a matter of indifference, even to we citizens on the frontier. If President McKinley succumbs to his wounds, the vice president must take over the reins of government. You know that. But we must hope the president survives, for I do not know if Vice President Chester Arthur is an honest man."

Sarah sighed, thinking of the far-off cities of the East, surrounded by green trees and mountains, full of people concerned with fashion and scandal. *All of that has little to do with us,* she thought.

"The railroad has already reached Deming, very close to us," Mama said, seeming to guess her thoughts. "We are much more connected to the affairs of the world now."

Maybe so. Sarah dropped her chin to the table. *But for now, I can think of nothing but the empty desert and my loss.*

The next day Sarah poked her needle carefully through the thick cotton of the quilt she, Mama, Mrs. Stauton, and Phoebe were making. Yellow morning sunshine flooded over the desert, warming Sarah's hands. Out by the big corral she could see Papa and Calvin Stauton doctoring an injured calf. Rachel looked over Papa's shoulder, stroking a copper-colored hen in her arms. The air hung still and calm, signifying a peaceful day.

"Well, it's fine to get together like this," Mrs. Stauton said, holding up her side of the quilt to examine her work. "I'm sure the quilt will find a use."

Sarah stopped sewing, and for a moment the flowered pattern of the quilt in front of her blurred. She knew what Mrs. Stauton meant. Several of the neighbors had advised against making the quilt for Zachary. If he died, as so many babies did, especially small ones, the quilt would just remind the family of their sorrow. Most families waited a year before they committed to a baby, but Sarah was glad Mama had insisted on making the quilt. *It is so beautiful,* Sarah thought, touching the stitchery of a pink rose lightly with her fingers. *Not rough-hewn, like so much else on the frontier. I do not have enough beauty in my life now that Moon Dancer is gone.*

Sarah rose, trying to collect her thoughts. *He has been gone for months,* she reminded herself. *If only I could stop dreaming that he is alive but hungry and mistreated.* "Would you care for some tea?" she asked Phoebe and her mother.

"Sure thing," said Phoebe, smiling. She nodded understandingly, as if she knew where Sarah's thoughts had been. Sarah smiled back gratefully. Phoebe seemed to have some idea of how terrible Sarah felt over the loss of her horse.

Late in the afternoon, the Stautons left to get home before dark, with time for chores. Sarah carefully folded the quilt, which was done except for the very end piece. She placed the quilt at the end of Zachary's crib, then carried the little teacups and plates to the sink and washed them while Mama fed Zachary. Soon Papa and Rachel would come in for supper. Standing beside her mother, Sarah looked out the window at the stark, strange landscape, so full of danger, now purpled with the shadows of dusk. *Where is my horse out there?* she wondered.

Mama laid Zachary in his cradle, which she had set on the kitchen table. "Let's tend to supper," she said. "I'll heat up a beef stew. Will you dig up potatoes and carrots from the garden?"

Sarah walked to the door but stopped with her hand on the latch. *I do not want to go out unless it is to search for my horse in that emptiness,* she thought. *But I fear it so.*

Zachary let out a little cry, and Sarah looked back at the tiny baby. "Mama, after all our troubles, do you think Papa will go back to Fort Smith?" she asked.

"No, because *I* don't want to go," Mama said firmly, stirring the stew with a wood spoon. "And neither does your father. It was my idea to come out here. Your father heard about this area from Uncle Matt, but I decided we should go."

Mama set down the spoon across the big iron pot and looked

directly at Sarah. "Daughter, Fort Smith was stifling. I know our lives are hard out here. But we're not *confined.* We don't have nosy neighbors watching what we do. The air is fresh, and we don't walk dirty streets every day. . . . I just wasn't surviving there. I lost all those babies, even though we had such a civilized life. Zachary was born alive out here, and he's doing just fine. This is home now."

Sarah stared at her mother. *I never guessed it was Mama's idea to come out here,* she said to herself. *I thought she liked being a fine lady!* "But the Apaches . . ." she began. "We can't live here with them around. They stole my horse. What will they take next?"

"Sarah, only a few vagabonds are left." Mama sighed. "They'll be on reservations soon enough. Of course they don't want to go there—they're confined, and they aren't treated kindly. This was once their land."

Sarah's head jerked up at the sound of soft thrumming across the desert. "Hoofbeats," she cried. "Mama, help—Papa and Rachel are out there!"

Mama crossed swiftly to the door and peeked out. "It's soldiers," she said. "Many of them. I wonder why they are out at night?"

Sarah heard the jingle of spurs, and her shoulders slumped with relief. Through the crack in the door she could see the soldiers dismounting from their horses and tying them to the posts of the new porch.

"Sarah?" Papa called. "Come outside—I have a wonderful surprise!"

No, it can't be, Sarah thought, but her heart thudded with hope. She tore out of the house and ran past the soldiers. Just behind the saddled army horses stood Papa, holding Moon Dancer by the reins.

"Oh, Dancer!" Sarah cried, rushing up to her horse. "It is you! I can hardly believe it. You're back!"

The pinto dropped his head into her arms and huffed out a

sweet breath. Sarah closed her eyes and hugged him, resting her cheek against his forehead. *You are real and came back to me,* she thought. *Never, ever disappear into the desert again.* Moon Dancer whickered, as if to reassure her.

"The soldiers found him some miles from here," Papa said. "I gather there was a battle with the Indians today, and the soldiers captured him from them."

"How did they know he was mine?" Sarah asked Papa.

"Miss, we didn't," said a tall man in uniform, stepping forward. "We just stopped by to make sure that your family was all right."

"This is Captain Smith," Papa said. "My daughter Sarah."

"Thank you so very much, Captain," Sarah said, her voice cracking.

"You're quite welcome," the captain replied. "We're glad we could return your property."

Sarah stepped back to examine her horse. "Papa, he's so thin," she whispered.

"He's lucky to be alive." Papa shook his head. "He can't have gotten much to eat if he's been running with the Apaches."

"He's still pretty," Rachel said from behind her.

Sarah turned to her sister, tears in her eyes. "Yes, he is," she said. "He's the most beautiful horse in the world. But—but Papa, what if the Apaches do come again? They took Moon Dancer once already. . . ."

"We'll stay the night, if you don't mind," Captain Smith said to Papa. "We can set up our tents outside. Your horse will be safe."

"We're much obliged," Papa said.

"Yes, we are." Sarah sighed. *I cannot possibly tell the captain how grateful I am,* she thought. *He has not only returned my horse, but my peace of mind.* "I'm going to feed Dancer," she said.

"Give him a ration of corn," Papa said with a smile.

Sarah led her horse toward the small corral. Moon Dancer followed without being asked, and as Sarah moved aside the boards to open the corral, she felt him blow out a soft sigh, as if he was relieved to be home.

"Let me feed you and brush you—oh, you're probably more thirsty than anything else," Sarah told the pinto as she slipped off his bridle. She picked up his long-empty water bucket. "But I'll fix everything now that you're back—I promise you will have a fine time here to make up for everything you have been through."

The pinto moved slowly around the corral, sniffing the fence. Sarah watched him a moment. He was definitely fit—more muscular than she had ever seen him. *At least he did not get sick, wherever he was,* she thought. *Thank God for that.* She lifted her eyes to the sky. The moon shone back, full and clear, bleaching the ground bone white.

"I would expect you to be back in the time of the full moon—you are definitely a moon horse," Sarah said as she replaced the gate to the corral. "That is a superstitious thought, and superstition is against the teachings of the church, but I can't help it."

Sarah quickly brought Moon Dancer water, grain, and hay, then had the satisfaction of seeing her horse hungrily munching his food. She lingered just a little while to run a soothing brush over his neck and sides. "I'd best go help Mama with our company," she said. "It's the least I can do, when they have brought you back to me."

Moon Dancer rolled an eye to look at her, but he didn't stop eating. Smiling blissfully, Sarah ran to the house.

The soldiers had made fires by the river. Sarah could hear snatches of conversation and song and the clatter of cookware as the men set up their tents and prepared their evening meal. *If only they could stay forever,* she thought.

When she opened the door to the kitchen, Mama was pouring

coffee into the china cups for the captain and two of his officers. "Sarah, this is Sergeant Dawes and Sergeant McFarland," Mama said. "Gentlemen, my daughter Sarah."

The two men half rose from their chairs. "Delighted, miss," said Sergeant Dawes, the younger of the two sergeants. He had blond hair and a darker blond beard. Sergeant McFarland appeared to be in his mid-thirties and had wavy brown hair. Both officers had thick mustaches that curled up at the ends.

"Where did your troop ride out from, Captain?" Papa asked.

"Fort Cummings." Captain Smith took a swallow of his coffee. "Excellent coffee, ma'am," he said to Mama. "Most appreciated. We've been on the trail for several weeks now."

"Where did the Apaches go?" Sarah couldn't help asking, although she didn't want to seem rude.

Captain Smith frowned. "We think into the upper reaches of Cooke's Peak again, although at least one party of them was headed this way."

"So you don't know how many there are," Papa said.

"Very few." Sergeant McFarland leaned forward. "Just a handful, I would guess."

"Soon the Indian threat will be over," Captain Smith said firmly.

I've heard that before, Sarah thought. *But just tonight I have seen seventy soldiers camping out by the river, and over many weeks they have not caught the Indians.*

"Tomorrow we ride back to the post, but a fresh regiment of soldiers will take over the search," Captain Smith said. "We will track them until we get them all."

Papa picked up the heavy iron coffeepot and refilled the men's cups.

"They are splendid warriors," said Sergeant Dawes, apparently noticing Sarah's expression. "They have little to eat and no comforts. How they have survived the onslaught of thousands of U.S. Army troops, I can scarcely imagine."

"Well, they will not continue to do so on my watch." Captain Smith set his cup down hard on the table.

"They must be subdued," Sergeant Dawes agreed.

The three officers declined Mama's offer of stew, saying they must rejoin their men. Papa saw the soldiers to the door, then helped Mama dish up and serve the meat, potatoes, and carrots. Either Mama or Papa must have dug up the carrots and potatoes for her, Sarah realized gratefully. Rachel came in from the living room, where she had been playing with Zachary. Mama set out butter and a loaf of bread, then poured milk for Sarah and Rachel. Papa retrieved Zachary from his cradle, and Mama held him in her lap while the family ate.

Sarah smiled at her little brother, but she could not get out of her mind her fear that the Apaches would be back. "How will the army subdue the Indians?" she asked.

"They must either be confined on reservations or killed," Papa said, breaking off a piece of bread. He rose, then came back with a match to light the kerosene lantern in the middle of the table. The flame sputtered, then caught on the wick.

"Is there no other way?" Mama looked sad. "They are God's creatures, just as we are."

"I don't see another solution," Papa replied. "But I do not pity them. They have inflicted much harm on the settlers."

I will be so frightened when the soldiers leave, Sarah thought, looking at her family, their faces aglow in the lantern's warm light. *What if we are attacked again?*

The next morning Sarah awoke at dawn, a strange dream still haunting her thoughts. The bedroom walls and floor were rosy brown with first light. Sarah groped under her bed for her diary.

August 19, 1881

Dear Diary,

I am awake, yet somehow still in the world of dreams. I dreamt I galloped Moon Dancer up that black and forbidding mountain to the east, Cooke's Peak. Perhaps I thought of it because the soldiers mentioned that was where they staged their battle with the Apaches yesterday. In the dream I rode Moon Dancer in the conflict, dodging bullets and arrows, the smell of gunpowder strong. I sought to escape, riding him hither and yon, but every time I tried to turn my horse away from the fight, we only confronted more soldiers and finally, the Apaches themselves.

The Apaches were not clear to my sight, for in real life I have never seen them. I know that they do not wear feather headdresses or clothes made of animal skins, as we were told in Fort Smith. In my dream they were simply a terrifying presence, forms without real shape, dark as rainclouds and as threatening. They drew closer, intending I knew not what. . . .

Sarah shook her head, trying to clear her mind. The rooster crowed outside, and Rachel stirred in the bed across the room, her glossy blond hair slipping over her face as she turned onto her stomach. *I'll go for a ride,* Sarah thought, setting her diary back under the bed and quickly gathering her clothes. As she passed through the kitchen she took a biscuit from the tin container for breakfast.

Outside in the yard, the soldiers had already left. The last curl of smoke from one of their fires arched into the still blue air of not yet morning. The sand was trampled with the marks of many hooves. *Although they protected us, still, this morning I am glad they are gone,* Sarah thought. *They remind me of war.*

Moon Dancer had dropped his head over the top board of the corral fence. He whinnied when he saw her. "Just a bite of breakfast for you before our ride," Sarah told him, walking to the barn to fetch him a sheaf of hay and get his tack. "We can both have a full breakfast later."

Sarah thought about her ride as she watched the pinto eat. "You have been with the Indians," she said. "I suppose I'll have to retrain you a great deal."

Moon Dancer snorted, then lipped up the last bit of hay. Sarah saddled and bridled him, then led him out of the corral. "I have an idea," she said, putting her foot in the stirrup and swinging quickly into the saddle. "I will let you go for a bit, and you can show me what you have been doing. Then I will begin to retrain you."

A fresh breeze caught her hair, pulling wisps of it from her braid. From her horse's back, Sarah looked across the flat, limitless space, capped by only the pale blue sky, and closed her eyes, smiling in sheer bliss. *I got my horse back!* she thought.

Moon Dancer pawed the ground, his dark eyes eager, his shoulder muscles bunching as he resisted the confining reins.

"Run!" Sarah cried.

The pinto raced straight out across the sand, his hooves kicking up clouds of dust. Sarah leaned forward, her cheek pressed to her horse's silken neck as he pounded toward the rising sun. Moon Dancer ran faster than ever before, but this time she let the reins slip through her fingers and didn't try to slow him. *Never have I felt so free, as if my horse and I were one perfect being,* she thought. *The light and strength of the sun and this land are mine as we run for glory.*

12

Gray-black clouds swept the silent, grim mountain, signs of an oncoming afternoon storm. Bin-daa-dee-nin climbed the steepest part of the mountain, near the top, his hands grasping the rough gray rocks, his feet searching for footholds. The ground was already damp from the rain-heavy clouds. But he moved quickly, his heart beating fast with hope. He had found a faint trail of his brothers at last.

Even with Bin-daa-dee-nin's great tracking skills, he had found no trace of them for the rising of many suns. Then suddenly, he had seen scraped dirt and a broken twig. The dirt had been pushed by a dragging boot. Although the soldiers and miners also wore boots, they would not be up this high on the mountain. *My time alone will end,* Bin-daa-dee-nin rejoiced, looking through the fingers of cloud. *I will not be here with no voice but my own.*

He saw a slight shift in the pattern of colors ahead, in front of a cliff face, and scrambled across loose boulders toward it, his feet light. Yuu-his-kishn stepped toward him from under a shelf of rock.

For an instant Bin-daa-dee-nin slowed, trying to understand what he saw. His brother's thin body, covered in ragged strips of cloth, hardly seemed his own. Then Nzhų-'a'c-siin stepped out from behind a rock and almost fell. "Brother," he croaked. Yuu-his-kishn grabbed his wrist to support him.

Bin-daa-dee-nin threw his arms around his brothers, his hands tight on their shoulders, letting strength return to him. *They live,* was all he could think. Then he looked again at Nzhų-'a'c-siin. His face was gray, and the bones of his chest showed through his skin like a skeleton's. Yuu-his-kishn followed his gaze.

"What should we do?" he asked quietly.

Bin-daa-dee-nin dropped his hands and began to pace. *We are hunted and trapped,* he thought. *I will not stay here and wait to be captured. Nzhų-'a'c-siin needs good food.*

"Where are the horses?" he asked.

"Gone," Yuu-his-kishn replied. "They ran away because they were starving. But we had no use for them up here."

"Then the soldiers have them." Bin-daa-dee-nin continued to walk; he could not make himself be still.

"Perhaps," said Nzhų-'a'c-siin, his voice broken. "Or they may have joined the herd of wild horses. Sometimes I have seen them in the distance. They are too clever for the soldiers to catch."

Bin-daa-dee-nin looked down the mountainside. From here, the short trees and cactus at the bottom were all humps of green scattered across the sand. *I know what I must do,* he thought. "If we have no horses, then I will have to run," he said.

"Where are you going?" Yuu-his-kishn demanded.

"Hunting," Bin-daa-dee-nin replied.

"Maybe you'll finally listen to me instead!" Yuu-his-kishn shouted. "We have to surrender and go on the reservation. Only three of us are left, and Nzhų-'a'c-siin is dying. We lost all our supplies."

Bin-daa-dee-nin turned and looked at the other Apaches.

"Why did you not go already?" he asked.

"We waited for you," Nzhų-'a'c-siin said. He sank to the ground. "We hoped you would find us."

"I have. Now I must go hunt." Bin-daa-dee-nin saw a rifle on the ground next to Nzhų-'a'c-siin and picked it up. Nzhų-'a'c-siin silently handed him three bullets.

"Where?" Yuu-his-kishn repeated.

"The ranch," Bin-daa-dee-nin answered, starting down the mountain. "I lost my horse. I'm going to get him back. Then I can go on better raids."

"You do not know that the horse is on the ranch," Yuu-his-kishn snapped. "You are just going to kill the ranchers for revenge. But they are all armed."

"If they come outside, I'll kill them," Bin-daa-dee-nin said grimly. *I know the horse is on that ranch,* he thought. *After the battle, the soldiers' dust went that way. Even if the soldiers did not take him, that is where he lives when he is not with me. He would have run there by himself.*

"Do you have a plan, or are you just going to get killed!" Yuu-his-kishn shouted.

Bin-daa-dee-nin paused. "I will get what supplies I can," he said. "Then I will take my horse. We can try to go to Mexico again."

"That won't work any better than it did the last time," Yuu-his-kishn said. "We have to—"

"I will not hear this," Bin-daa-dee-nin said furiously, plunging down into the boulder field. He let his speed and rage slide him down it until he reached the first of the tiny trees that grew on the mountain and a narrow deer path. *I must get my horse again,* he thought. *Only then will our lives be better.*

Rain began to pelt his head and shoulders when he reached the foot of the mountain. The light left quickly, covered by clouds.

Bin-daa-dee-nin ran across the wet, dark sand, his footsteps swift and steady, eating up the ground. *I do not want to get killed,* he said to himself. *My brother is right that the ranchers will fight me. But there is only one man to shoot. The woman and two girls will not attack.*

Thunder cracked open the sky, and a white stick of lightning struck the ground close by, catching a mesquite tree on fire. The yellow flames burned along its branches, a fiery skeleton in the gloom.

Bin-daa-dee-nin glanced at the sky. To the west he saw deep, pink feathers of cloud on a night blue sky. The rain would not last long. He wished that it would so that he would have better cover. Soon the moon would rise as well, lighting the whole desert with its brilliant eye.

I will make the rancher think a whole band of Apaches is attacking, Bin-daa-dee-nin thought. *That is how I will be careful of my life.*

13

We paused before a House that seemed
A swelling of the Ground—
The Roof was scarcely visible—
The Cornice—in the Ground—

Sarah turned a page in her handwritten collection of Emily Dickinson's poems, bending forward so that the firelight from the living room hearth fell on the words. Emily Dickinson was a friend of one of Mama's acquaintances in Fort Smith, and Mama's friend had gotten a copy of the poems from the shy poet.

Since then—'tis Centuries—and yet
Feels shorter than the Day
I first surmised the Horses' Heads
Were toward Eternity—

Sarah glanced over at Zachary, who slept in his crib with a tiny fist to his mouth, then looked out the window. *The moon is full,* she thought uneasily. *I do not believe in werewolves or other ghostly visitations in the dark, but I cannot help feeling that tonight I must be extra watchful.*

Rachel stretched out on her stomach across from Sarah on

the hearth, puzzling over a primer, her golden curls falling across her face. Mama had gone to bed early, and Papa sat across from the girls in the rocker, repairing a bridle.

Bang. A stone hit the tin roof of the house. Sarah started to her feet in alarm, the book sliding to the floor. "What was that?" she cried.

Outside, she heard the shuffle of the cattle moving around in the big corral, then the lowing of several cows. Moon Dancer whinnied from the small corral.

"Indians!" Sarah cried. "They're after my horse again!"

"They're after whatever they can find." Mr. Chilton grabbed his rifle from the table by his chair and ran outside.

Sarah rushed to the door and looked out. Near the chicken house she could just make out a dark, running shape. The chickens squawked. "Not my chickens!" Rachel wailed. One chicken made a strangled, choking cry. "No!" Rachel screamed. Pushing by Sarah, she raced out the door.

"Rachel!" *Dear God, she just signed her own death warrant,* Sarah thought, gathering her skirt and running after her sister. Sarah stopped short just in front of the chicken house, her hand to her mouth, staring in horror at the awesome, frightful scene before her.

A young Indian loomed over Rachel, who was crouched on the ground, holding a chicken in her arms. The Indian had the butt of his gun raised and was about to club her. The anger and ferocity on his face were terrifying.

Time seemed to have stopped. Her sister and the Indian stared at each other, but Rachel wasn't crying or moving an inch.

The Indian raised the gun higher. *Run, Rachel!* Sarah thought frantically. Suddenly a shot rang out from by the house. Whipping her head around, Sarah saw Papa sighting along his gun.

The Indian took a shot back at Mr. Chilton, who ducked around the house. Sarah clutched her ears. A bullet hit the ground with a slap of dust at the Indian's feet. Sarah ran across the yard and pulled Rachel to her feet.

"Come with me!" Sarah cried, dragging her to Papa. Out of the corner of her eye she could see Moon Dancer racing madly around the corral. Sarah saw the Indian start in his direction, but Papa's rifle warned him off.

"Get in the house, girls!" Papa cried, running for the door.

In the kitchen Mama held Zachary in her arms, her forehead creased with worry. "Thank God you're safe," she said. "Rachel, do not on any condition leave this house again."

Rachel, stroking the bronze feathers of her softly clucking chicken, did not reply.

Papa peered out into the night from the doorway. "I do not see them," he said at last.

"Maybe they've run off," Sarah said weakly.

A stone clattered down the roof again. Sarah screamed—she couldn't help it. *Will they massacre us?* she thought.

Mr. Chilton grabbed her by the shoulders. "Sarah, you must ride to get the soldiers at Fort Cummings. It's but an hour's ride. Otherwise we may not survive this raid—the Indians may burn the house."

"I—I can't, Papa," Sarah whispered. She clasped her hands, trying to stop their trembling, but shivers shook her entire body.

"Look at me." Papa lifted Sarah's chin until she met his gaze. She saw fear in his dark eyes but also fierce determination. "You're our best rider," he said. "I wouldn't ask it if I didn't know that you could." Papa tossed a rifle to Mama and handed the bridle he had been mending to Sarah. "I'll cover you as you run to the corral. Go, now!"

Mama stepped to the door, holding the rifle aloft, her face

grim. "God be with you, Sarah," she said quietly.

"Mama . . ." But Papa was pushing Sarah out the door. She tripped over her skirt and almost fell.

"Hurry," Papa whispered. "Before they guess our purpose."

In a daze Sarah ran to the corral, her boots sinking into the sand, fumbling with the straps of the bridle. It was not Moon Dancer's, and she tried to adjust it so that it would fit him. Papa followed her with the gun raised.

Moon Dancer was trotting around the corral. When he saw them, he stopped, snorted, then trotted off again.

Sarah climbed up the fence, vaulted over the top board, and dropped into the corral. She forced herself to approach the excited horse slowly, with one hand outstretched. Moon Dancer shot by her, kicking up his heels, and Sarah swallowed hard. "Come here, boy," she whispered. Moon Dancer stopped and cocked his head, and Sarah quickly put her hand on his shoulder before he could think about running again. She bridled the horse with trembling hands, then looked toward the fence. Papa was struggling to hang on to his rifle and pull out the boards so that Sarah could ride Moon Dancer through. *I've only a bridle, no saddle,* she thought. In the gleam of the moonlight Moon Dancer was prancing in place, barely holding still. *Can I even get on? I have to!*

Gripping Moon Dancer's mane, Sarah jumped as high as she could and tried to throw her boot over his back. Pushing off the fence with her other leg, she straddled the horse.

A shot whistled by her foot and Sarah bit her tongue. She tried to push images of a shattered leg from her mind. If she became any more terrified, she wouldn't be able to move. Papa almost had the top board removed from the fence.

Sarah saw a shadow in the moonlight, coming toward the corral, and fought back a scream. *I can't wait for Papa to get the gate open,* she thought. She wheeled Moon Dancer, the horse light under her hands, and pointed him at the corral fence. "If that Apache can jump the fence, so can I," she whispered, but her whole body shook with fear. Sarah clapped her heels into the pinto's sides. "Go, Dancer!" she cried.

Moon Dancer bounded forward. *Don't refuse . . . don't refuse . . .* Sarah prayed. The pinto gathered his legs under him, then lifted. Sarah felt them go airborne, soaring toward the moon. She clung to the horse's sides with her legs. If she fell, it was certain death at the Apache's hands. But Moon Dancer cleared the fence with ease. Sarah grabbed his mane again as they hit the sand with a thud and straightened herself on his back.

A shape was running after her in the dark. *He's coming after me!* Sarah realized, her heart thundering. *He wants the horse!* She had never seen anyone run so fast.

Moon Dancer hesitated and looked back. "Go!" Sarah screamed. "Don't stop!" She slapped Moon Dancer's rump with the reins. Finally he began to trot, then broke into a quick gallop. Sarah checked their direction—the moon, high above, should be just east as they headed in the direction of Cooke's Peak. The fort was a few miles south of there.

Sarah urged Moon Dancer across the open desert, pushing him on with her hands and legs, fear for her family overpowering her thoughts. Moon Dancer was running fast, occasionally throwing up his head, his hoofbeats staccato on the sand.

She had not been out in the desert at night since she had found her horse so many months ago. The bright ground seemed covered with white crystals of snow, crunching quickly under Moon Dancer's hooves. The cactus and rocks, directly under the moon, kept their shadows to themselves. *Thank goodness I can see obstacles,* Sarah thought. *I must not fall now.*

The desert was utterly still around them, unbroken by sound or movement. She and Moon Dancer were completely alone in a vast, old world, isolated from time. *Moon Dancer and I seem a part of the desert, as much as the sand and cactus, and bound together in the same way,* Sarah thought. *We belong here and will not fail.*

After a couple of miles she forced herself to ease up on Moon Dancer, sitting back until he slowed to a rocking, steady gallop. *Nothing will be gained by killing the horse,* she told herself. They should reach the fort soon.

On the horizon she saw a group of animals moving quickly toward her. Moon Dancer saw them too and pricked his ears. "Antelope?" Sarah murmured, gripping the pinto's mane tightly. Voices floated toward her on the still night air, and Sarah slumped with relief. In her experience, Apaches didn't travel in big, slow-moving groups. "It's soldiers."

Two riders detached from the main body of the troop and rode toward her. "Hello!" Sarah shouted before colorful Moon Dancer could be mistaken for an Indian pony.

"What's your business?" called back one of the soldiers.

Sarah rode up to him and quickly described the attack on her home. "We'll accompany you back," said the soldier, stroking his mustache. He turned to the other man. "Private, get the men up here."

On the ride to the ranch Sarah dropped to the back of the troop. These were different soldiers from the other night—she didn't see Captain Smith or any of his men. Moon Dancer easily kept up with the slow gallop of the troop's horses. Fragments of conversation and a snatch of smoke from a cigarette floated back to her. *Can't the soldiers ride any faster?* she thought. *God only knows what is happening at the ranch.*

When they finally reached the ranch, Sarah flung herself off

Moon Dancer and ran to the house. Her heart hammering, she yanked open the door. *Please let me not find a scene of blood and death,* she prayed. “Papa? Mama?” she called.

“We’re fine,” Mama said, coming out of the living room, holding Zachary. Rachel followed her with her chicken, which was now asleep, its head tucked into its breast. “We weren’t attacked again,” Mama reassured Sarah.

Sarah sank into a chair, letting her face drop into her hands. She could feel the grit from her long ride on her skin. “Thank God,” she said, hardly able to believe the good news.

One of the soldiers’ horses whinnied from outside, and Sarah sat up straight. “I’ve got to feed Dancer,” she said.

“I can do that for you,” Papa offered.

“No, I will. Thank you, Papa.” Sarah stood up shakily. Her legs were still trembling from strain.

“All right.” Papa squeezed her shoulder. “That was fine riding tonight, my dear.”

Moon Dancer stood in the yard where she had left him. As Sarah approached, he whinnied softly.

Sarah dropped her hand to his shoulder, overwhelmed with love for her horse. “You’re always there when I need you,” she said. “And you always do what needs to be done. I’d say tonight you have earned your feed.”

The pinto followed her eagerly to the corral. Sarah slipped off his bridle and fetched him hay and a little grain from the barn. “Not too much,” she said as she dropped the green sheaf of hay in front of him. “I don’t want you to colic after all that exertion.”

“Sarah!” Mama called from the house.

Sarah gave her horse one last pat. “Who knows, I might take to riding without a saddle,” she said with a smile. “I would not have expected it, but I actually found staying on bareback easier.”

On her way to the house she passed the soldiers. They had dismounted from their horses. *I wonder if they will spend the night again?* she thought. *I will be very glad if they do.*

Up at the house Mama had set out a bowl and a glass of milk on the table. "Eat, Sarah," she said. "It's been a long night for you."

Sarah was almost too tired to know what she was eating—some kind of vegetables and pork, maybe. Mama would have had to trade something to one of the neighbors for pork since the Chiltons didn't keep pigs. Sarah realized her mind was wandering. Her eyes drifted closed.

Hoofbeats pounded across the desert. Sarah's eyes flew open, and she leapt to her feet. Papa was already running outside.

It's too late, Sarah thought. From the doorway she could see the Apache boy riding Moon Dancer off into the moonlit desert, fleeing toward Cooke's Peak. The soldiers were shouting and rushing to their horses, but Sarah knew the boy was long gone. *What will he do now?* she wondered, dazed. *I hope he knows enough not to run Moon Dancer to death. The soldiers will be furious that he stole the horse right out from under their noses. They'll pursue him to the ends of the earth this time.*

Papa stomped back into the house and slammed the door. "I'm joining up with the army." Papa's face was grim. "I'm going to stop those thieving Apaches once and for all."

"No, Papa, don't leave!" Sarah begged, horrified. "What if the Apaches come back?"

"They won't come back—there's nothing left for them to take," Papa said bitterly.

Except our lives, Sarah thought. But she knew in her heart that the Apaches didn't come to kill, only to steal. "But—but how long will you be gone?" she asked, running after her father as he picked up his rifle. *He can't just leave us alone!*

"I'll be back soon—we're getting reinforcements from Fort Bayard. Sarah, take care of your mother and sister and the baby. I can ask the Stautons to send over Calvin."

"No, we'll be all right," Mama said forcefully. "If twenty of them come, Calvin won't make a difference."

"Papa—be careful," Sarah whispered. *I think I alone know just how desperate the Apaches are.*

14

The next morning Sarah opened the door a crack, then stepped outside, stretching her stiff limbs. What little sleep she had gotten had been sitting up—she had slept with her head on the kitchen table, Papa's pistol by her hand. All night she'd started awake at every little noise, imagining the Apaches had come back to kill them all. Then she'd worried about Papa and Moon Dancer: they might get shot. Toward dawn, half asleep, she'd fretted about how to take care of everybody and the ranch. Suppose Zachary died?

The sun bathed her face in glorious warmth, and Sarah fell to her knees in the sand, her terrors of the night gone. "Thank you, God, for this beautiful day," she said softly. "And that we have all lived to see it."

The soldiers were skilled fighters, and Moon Dancer had come to her twice before. *He will be back,* Sarah thought. *I know it.*

Mama joined her, holding Zachary. Sarah was relieved to see her little brother's pink cheeks and alert expression. He reached out a determined hand for her hair. "Let's decide what needs to be done today, Sarah," Mama said.

Sarah nodded, tilting her head away from Zachary's hand and letting him have her finger instead. Her mind began to work. First there were the cows to feed. Ordinarily they would be let out to forage, but she did not want them to fall prey to the raiders. *I will keep them in the corral and feed them hay for three days and see if Papa returns,* she thought. *If he doesn't, I'll let them out anyway.*

"I'm going to can tomatoes today," said Mama. "That will give us a start on our winter provisions."

"I'll feed the cattle and then help you." Sarah pushed loose strands of hair out of her eyes and headed for the big corral. She'd tend to personal grooming later.

Rachel hurried across the yard. "And where are you going, young lady?" Mama asked.

Rachel turned around and walked backward. "The chicken coop needs cleaning."

"Tend to your chickens, then report back to me," Mama told her sternly. "With Papa gone, you'll have to do more chores, Rachel."

Rachel saluted, and Sarah smiled. "You've been around the soldiers too much," she said.

"I like the soldiers." Rachel tossed her curls. "One of them said I was a cutie."

"Well, you are," Sarah said absently, her thoughts on the day ahead. "The cattle are the main chore," she said aloud.

Mama nodded. "Go and tend to them. If you need help, let me know."

In the big corral, the cows were mooing and shuffling around, pushing one another. They stared at Sarah with their big brown eyes. Sarah frowned.

"I don't know why I thought I could feed you hay—you'd clean out every bale in the barn in no time," she said. "You'll have to forage, and when Papa comes back, he can round you up. Or if he is away a long time . . ." Sarah didn't want to think about that. "The neighbors can help me round you up."

Before she let the cattle out, Sarah looked them over, the way Papa would, for wounds or sickness. Luckily they all seemed in good health. "You're rather pretty, in a cow kind of way," Sarah told them, admiring the animals' shiny black coats. "Time to eat—I'm sure you're ready for that."

She opened the boards of the corral and the cattle streamed out past her, scattering across the range. As she walked by the smaller corral, Sarah looked at the fence in wonder—the top board was almost as high as her head. "How did I manage to jump that last night?" she said.

Sarah dusted off her hands. Papa spent much of the day fixing things, but most of that could wait for his return. Hopefully they wouldn't need provisions from Silver City until then. *Helping Mama prepare food for the winter is the best expenditure of my time today,* she decided.

Back at the house, Mama had laid out a long row of glass jars. Tomatoes, plums, peaches, and green beans were piled on the kitchen table. Pinto beans and almonds, which didn't have to be preserved, were already carefully stowed in larger jars, protected from rats and mice.

Mama cooked down the fruits and vegetables on the stove, and Sarah poured them into jars, carefully sealed them with wax, and set the jars on the kitchen shelves. Rachel joined them a little later, helping to clean up the sticky juice that fell on the stove and floor and handing Sarah jars.

Mama began to sing a hymn they'd often sung at church in Fort Smith. Sarah glanced sideways at her mother. *Mama hasn't sung in a long time,* she realized. Sarah was thankful that her mother felt well enough to do this hot, demanding work: she'd been standing most of the day. Zachary, propped up with pillows on a chair, watched them work with wide, bright eyes. *I think things are going to be all right.* Sarah smiled, feeling her shoulders relax as if an actual weight had been lifted.

The day passed quickly, and as the sun set, a glowing ball on the western horizon, Sarah put the last jar of plums on the shelf.

"That's it for this batch," Mama said, wiping her forehead on her sleeve. "We'll do more tomorrow."

"I'll climb the trees and pick more almonds," Rachel volunteered.

I managed, Sarah thought, smiling at her little sister. *We all did. Papa would be proud.*

The sun disappeared, and pink puffs of cloud slowly faded as shadow advanced from the east. Sarah shivered as she helped Rachel lay out the plates for dinner. She tried to hold her fears at bay, but the darkness had caused them to return. Papa was out there somewhere in the night, riding with the soldiers. She and her mother and sister were alone at the ranch.

Sarah's hands stopped moving the plates. She squeezed her eyes shut, trying to suppress the thought, but it forced itself into her mind anyway. *What if Papa doesn't come back?*

15

Bin-daa-dee-nin sat quietly on his horse, looking out over the desert from the mountaintop. Summer would soon be over—he could feel it in the chill edging the night air, the old age of the deep green, insect-bitten leaves, the sigh in the wind as the spirit of summer departed. *Everything is ending,* he thought.

Nzhų-'a'c-siin and Yuu-his-kishn slept, their backs against the cliff where he had left them. They were so thin and tired. If the soldiers came now, he doubted his brothers could run far.

Moon That Flies dropped his head and looked back at him. The horse's sweet, gentle gaze stirred Bin-daa-dee-nin's sad heart. *Truly your kindness is a precious gift,* he thought. *I have you, at this moment, and that is a great good.*

But he could not help thinking of what was to come. Death? The reservation? He tried to imagine life on the reservation: the sickness, cold, and despair. "I may not be allowed to live," he said aloud. "Perhaps it is better to die now, while I am free."

Moon That Flies flicked back an ear, listening. Bin-daa-dee-nin leaned forward and hugged the horse's neck, breathing in his comforting animal smell and letting his fur tickle his arms. He sat back up, suddenly angry.

I will live, he told himself fiercely. *In some way. I will never be broken at the reservation.*

"But what of you?" he said softly to his horse. "Such a fine animal should not be doing foolish work on a ranch or in the army, work that any mule or inferior horse could do. No rancher or soldier is deserving of you."

He remembered the raid three nights ago, when he had gotten back Moon That Flies. The ranch girl had jumped the corral fence with his horse and galloped off into the night. He had not seen a girl in a long dress ride with such determination and courage that way before.

I thought she would fall off after the jump, he thought. *Then Moon That Flies almost waited for me.* But the horse had obeyed his rider. It had served the girl well in making her escape.

Moon That Flies started down the mountain. Bin-daa-dee-nin did not ask him where they were going. He leaned back, half closing his eyes, loving the surefooted animal's easy gait. After the last raid, as the moon set, he and his brothers had roasted the two chickens he'd taken from the ranch. Now they all felt stronger, although they had not eaten much since. Bin-daa-dee-nin remembered that strange little girl, guarding her chicken. *She had luck,* he thought. *I almost killed her. I could see in her face she knew—but she was still unafraid. She was like an Apache girl, angry and fighting in the face of death. Then that man shot at me—*

The crack of a rifle jerked him upright, as if his thoughts had caused it to appear. A bullet slapped onto nearby rock, splintering it into gray shards.

Soldiers! Bin-daa-dee-nin realized. *This is revenge for the raid.*

Bin-daa-dee-nin wheeled Moon That Flies and took off through the short trees. *I must lead them away from my brothers,* he thought. He found a natural trail for his escape, a ledge around the mountain. Bin-daa-dee-nin galloped Moon That Flies until the ledge dropped off, then glanced back. He almost cried out. The soldiers were so close, he could see their faces. And they were not just soldiers—ranchers were there as well. *I cannot lose them,* he thought. *They know this mountain too well—as well as I do. It is now their mountain.* A bitter taste filled Bin-daa-dee-nin's mouth. *But even if I am caught and killed, perhaps my brothers escaped.*

Moon That Flies suddenly jumped downhill, leaving the trail. Bin-daa-dee-nin let the reins go slack to give the horse his head. Moon That Flies pushed through a thicket, then picked his way carefully across a small slide of rocks. Bin-daa-dee-nin's heart lifted. They would be hard to track on the rocks.

The sounds of pursuit faded. A strange quiet settled over the woods, as if spirits lurked and had silenced the animals and plants. He and Moon That Flies seemed to be the only living things in this unnatural world.

Bin-daa-dee-nin dropped his head. "You who are sent from the gods, guide me," he said softly. "For I do not know what to do."

When he looked up at last, he saw that his horse had led him back to where they had started on this mountain—there was the miners' wrecked wagon up ahead. Bin-daa-dee-nin slid off his horse and walked over to the wagon, feeling like he was in a dream but that someone was watching it, guiding his actions. He climbed onto the wagon bed and pushed aside the tattered canvas. The thick bars of silver were still there, shining dully in the last light of day. Grain and coffee spilled out of holes in the cloth sacks gnawed by mice. Laboriously Bin-daa-dee-nin began unloading bars of silver from the wagon, tossing them to the ground. After he had a big pile, he used a rock to dig and buried the bars under an ancient, spreading juniper that had somehow lived to be much older than the surrounding trees.

Just as he had hidden the last of the bars, he heard the crackle of underbrush and the shouts of his pursuers. Bin-daa-dee-nin surveyed his work calmly, critically. No sign of disturbance showed on the forest floor. Someday he would come back for this white man's treasure.

Bin-daa-dee-nin rested his hand on Moon That Flies' shoulder. His horse leaned into him, relaxed, seeming to know that their task was done.

At the sound of heavy footsteps, Bin-daa-dee-nin turned. The soldiers and ranchers were thick upon the mountain and coming toward him.

His hands bound behind his back, Bin-daa-dee-nin struggled to keep his balance as one of the soldiers on horseback dragged him down the mountain with a rope tied around his waist, following a long column of soldiers. Bin-daa-dee-nin tried to keep Moon That Flies in sight, but the horse soon disappeared among the marching men.

Darkness filled the sky as the soldiers reached the flickering fires of their camp at the bottom of the mountain. One soldier untied Bin-daa-dee-nin's rope and shoved him sideways into someone. Bin-daa-dee-nin looked up and saw Yuu-his-kishn. *He lives!* Bin-daa-dee-nin rejoiced. But Yuu-his-kishn's hands were bound. He was also a prisoner.

Bin-daa-dee-nin's relief turned to dread. *His imprisonment is my doing,* he thought. *He would not be here if we had done as he wished and gone back to the reservation. I will see his hatred.*

The two Apaches' eyes met, and Bin-daa-dee-nin saw quick joy in his brother's expression. Then Yuu-his-kishn nodded slightly, firmly.

Bin-daa-dee-nin nodded back, happiness filling his heart.

We will survive this together or die bravely, he told himself. *It is the Apache way.*

Yuu-his-kishn's gaze broke away from his. Bin-daa-dee-nin followed his look across the clearing.

Nzhų-'a'c-siin lay dying on the ground. A pool of blackening blood spread under his back, and one hand clutched his chest. His other hand gripped his rifle. A soldier standing beside him lifted his own rifle and pointed it at Nzhų-'a'c-siin's head.

Before he could cock the rifle, Bin-daa-dee-nin rushed across the clearing. He heard Yuu-his-kishn shout something in English, but the soldier leveled his rifle at Bin-daa-dee-nin anyway. Bin-daa-dee-nin ignored him and knelt by Nzhų-'a'c-siin, cradling his head in his hands. Nzhų-'a'c-siin 's eyes were closed, but then they opened and looked right at Bin-daa-dee-nin.

"Do not grieve for me," Nzhų-'a'c-siin said softly. "I am glad I got to die in battle."

"I am too." Bin-daa-dee-nin could not hide his terrible sorrow. Tears dropped onto Nzhų-'a'c-siin's face.

Nzhų-'a'c-siin lifted one hand to Bin-daa-dee-nin's cheek and smiled. "Do not forget your promise—to tell the old stories."

"I will not forget, brother." Bin-daa-dee-nin tried to make his expression strong and reassuring. Nzhų-'a'c-siin would not go into the afterlife with a last memory of sadness.

"Good." Nzhų-'a'c-siin's smile faltered, and his hand dropped to his side.

Bin-daa-dee-nin rested his forehead against his dead brother's warm chest. He could feel the spirits of the dead crowding around him, and this time he did not try to brush them back. Some had the vague faces of people he had known long ago: his mother and his father, a wise old medicine woman. The spirits twisted before him like smoke, beckoning with wispy fingers.

The point of a bayonet in his side yanked him from his thoughts. Bin-daa-dee-nin rose to face the soldiers and meet his own fate.

A full moon slipped over the black shoulder of the mountain, its light seeping over the rocks, then flooding the wide expanse of desert. The cactus were silent sentinels, dark in a river of white.

Bin-daa-dee-nin saw Moon That Flies, his legs restrained by hobbles, at the edge of the camp. The horse stood alone, away from the soldiers' mounts. Moon That Flies was watching him with his quiet gaze, his black patches fading into the night, his white glowing under the moon. Bin-daa-dee-nin returned his look, allowing his hunger for his horse to burn within him.

Gods of this place, do not let him come to harm, Bin-daa-dee-nin prayed. *For although he is your gift, he is only a horse and feels as I do. Let him find food and a dwelling of safety and love. For he has become one with me in spirit, and our spirits cannot rest unless it is together.*

16

SARAH PACED THROUGH THE HOUSE, twisting her fingers and peering out the kitchen window, then crossing to the living room window. She was all alone. Sarah had talked Mama into going to bed early with Zachary, pointing out just how much they had all gotten done today: the winter canning, the clothes washed and dried, five loaves of fresh bread baked. Rachel had refused to lie down in her own bed and had fallen asleep on the hearth, in front of the fire. Sarah was far too worried to sleep.

She sat in the rocker and picked up a torn sock to mend. But she couldn't concentrate, and after a few stitches she put the sewing aside and reached for her diary.

September 11, 1881

Dear Diary,

Papa has been gone with the soldiers for three days, and I have taken care of the ranch in his absence. We are all still alive. I have gotten used to my routine of chores and responsibilities, but I dread the coming of winter. Whatever shall I do without Papa? I do not want to frighten Mama by bringing up the possibility that we will have to manage alone. But of course she must be well aware of this. I think I do not want to frighten myself. . . .

At the sound of a clatter in the yard, Sarah jerked upright and dropped her pen. Her hand went to Papa's pistol on the chair beside her and she tiptoed to the door, her knees wobbly. *Please let this not be my greatest challenge yet,* Sarah prayed. *I cannot stave off an attack alone.*

Opening the door a crack, she poked the pistol out and looked into the yard. A large posse of men rode up on horses. Sarah slumped against the doorjamb in relief. The soldiers had returned. She stepped outside, eagerly searching the crowd for Papa.

Captain Smith trotted past her on his horse, then sharply pulled his mount to a halt. Sarah's hand flew to her mouth in shock. An Indian boy was tied with a rope to the horn of the saddle. He stumbled to a stop, his black hair falling over his face.

"Sarah!" called a familiar voice.

Sarah spun around. Her heart filled with gladness as she saw her father among the men. "Oh, Papa!" Sarah ran over to him and hugged him tight. "You're safe!"

"And you too." Papa hugged her back. "Is everyone well?"

"Just fine." Sarah could hardly speak. She never wanted to let Papa go.

"Look who's with me." Papa pointed behind him. A young soldier was holding a horse . . .

"Moon Dancer!" Sarah cried. The pinto eagerly lifted his head at the sound of her voice. Sarah rushed over to him, laughing from sheer happiness.

She quickly looked him over, worried that his strenuous adventures had harmed him. "You're not even winded," she said with relief. "I have to say, you're one tough horse. The only thing wrong with you is that your tail is full of cactus spines."

Moon Dancer tossed his black head, seeming unconcerned. "I'll fix you up," Sarah promised him, and kissed his nose.

Captain Smith pushed the Indian boy forward. He almost fell again, then looked up. He stared straight at Sarah and Moon Dancer.

The moonlight shone on his face, and Sarah could see him clearly. *He's the one who almost killed Rachel, the one who shot at us and took my horse,* she thought in surprise.

She realized the boy wasn't looking at her—just at Moon Dancer. Suddenly Sarah knew why he stole her horse and kept coming back for him. *It's his horse too,* she thought. *And not just a horse he rides to get places, like the soldiers. Moon Dancer is his the same way he's mine.* Sarah narrowed her eyes, trying to understand. *So he feels as I do. But he's going to the reservation. What will that be like—with no horse and home?*

The Apache boy looked steadily at Moon Dancer, but his black eyes gave nothing away.

He wants the horse back. Sarah stepped protectively closer to Moon Dancer. The pinto nudged her hands, tickling them with his whiskers. Apparently he hadn't forgotten that she usually had a treat for him. Sarah touched his soft nose, smiling. Moon Dancer whickered and tucked his head affectionately under her arm.

When Sarah looked up, something had changed in the Apache boy's expression, but she wasn't sure what it was. She found she could meet his gaze. *I'm not afraid anymore,* she realized. *Not of him, or the night, or loss . . . I will persevere and pull through. All of us on the ranch will.*

Mama had come out of the house with Rachel and Zachary. Sarah felt Mama's hand on her shoulder. Rachel patted Moon Dancer's flank. She didn't seem surprised to see him.

The soldiers mounted their horses again. "Good night to you," Captain Smith said, tipping his hat. "I do not expect we will meet again for a while."

"Thank you, Captain," Papa said.

Captain Smith swung up on his horse and gave the rope around the Apache boy a yank. *Will he have to go on foot all the miles to the post?* Sarah wondered. *How will he survive?*

She watched them go until the procession disappeared into the shadows. Miraculously the boy did not fall. *Perhaps he will not survive,* she thought. *But he did not beg for mercy or collapse—he must be very strong.*

"Put the horse in the corral and come inside, Sarah," Papa said.

"We have a lot to talk about," Mama added with a smile.

"I'll be in shortly," Sarah assured them. Her parents, sister, and brother returned to the house, and soon the glow of the lamp appeared in the kitchen window. Sarah remained outside with her horse, the moonlight bright upon them both, until the last hoofbeats disappeared in the east.

Epilogue

"CAR KEYS, CAR KEYS," sixteen-year-old Lindsay Summers muttered, rummaging through a pile of CDs, necklaces, and sunflower seeds on top of the dresser in her bedroom. She had to meet her two best friends, Kendra Stockton and Brittany Kohler, at Kendra's house in five minutes so that they could cheer on their friends at the high school basketball game.

With a bang the old picture on her dresser of her great-great-grandmother, Sarah Chilton, fell over. "Sorry, Grandma," Lindsay said, propping the picture back up. Sarah gazed back at her from the daguerreotype, her expression sweet, earnest, and a little sad. Lindsay knew that her grandmother was about Lindsay's age when the picture was taken, and Lindsay knew something of her grandmother's experiences: the death of her beloved little sister at age eight from measles, Sarah's pride years later when her brother, Zachary, became sheriff of Grant County, and a legendary pinto Sarah had that for twenty years could outrun any horse in the county. Then one day the horse disappeared—went back to the mountains or something, according to the old story.

Lindsay smiled at the picture of her grandmother. *She sure was pretty,* she thought.

She glimpsed her car keys sticking out behind a bud vase on her nightstand. "Yes!" Lindsay grabbed the keys and flew through the kitchen, snatching her windbreaker from a hook beside the door as she rushed outside to her dad's truck. The early February day had been warm and springlike, but the evening would be cool. Lindsay tossed the jacket onto the seat beside her, then carefully backed the truck around, watching for stray chickens and peacocks. *I'm an expert at animal control,* she thought. *Well, I ought to be.* She'd lived on the ranch, which had been in the family since the time of Grandma Sarah, all her life.

"Hi, Lindsay!" Kendra and Brittany were waiting in front of Brittany's house, waving. Plump, red-haired Kendra barely reached tall Brittany's shoulder.

They don't seem mad because I'm late, Lindsay thought with relief, stopping the truck abruptly in front of her friends. *I guess they're used to it.*

Brittany and Kendra ran to the truck and hopped in, pushing over on the bench seat. Kendra threw Lindsay's jacket in the back and bounced up and down. "Hurry up," Brittany urged, leaning around Kendra. "We're going to miss when the players run out on the court. I promised Kyle Richards that I'd stand up and cheer for him." She shook her dark bangs out of her eyes and held her hands up in the prayer position.

"Okay, okay." Lindsay shifted the truck into first gear, then whacked the steering wheel in frustration. "This thing's almost out of gas!"

"Oh no!" Kendra cried. "God, Lindsay, we're doomed." She giggled.

"It'll just take a minute to fill up." Lindsay quickly shifted the old truck's gears and got them traveling rapidly along one of the back roads to the school. She pulled into an isolated station at the edge of the desert and stuck the gas nozzle into the tank, ignoring her friends, who were loudly complaining about what a bad chauffeur she was.

Mike Torres looked into his rearview mirror and brushed back his black hair with one hand. *I guess I look okay,* he thought. *At least for a high school basketball game.* His friend Joe Richardson wanted to go to the game and look up old friends, even though both of them had graduated last year and high school kids were a little unsophisticated for them. Mike was in his second semester at Texas Tech, studying engineering, and Joe was at the University of New Mexico in the architecture program. Joe's dad was a professor of architecture at the university, and Joe was following in his footsteps. But Mike was the first college man in his family.

Mike pulled his Toyota Corolla into a gas station to get a soda. He was meeting Joe over at the school, and he would probably be late, but his family had kept him at home, catching up with him on all the news. Mike hadn't returned to his family's small house near Deming since Christmas, and his dad had wanted to show him the garage he'd built. Mike knew that his mother and father were very proud of owning their house, another sign of their success after generations of hard times.

The rez wasn't so good a hundred years ago, Mike thought. He'd heard the family stories about it. His great-great-grandfather Bin-daa-dee-nin was forced to surrender to the army and was dragged behind a horse to the Mescalero reservation near Fort Stanton. He had almost starved the next winter, but luckily in the confusion of many people from many places, no one had found out that he fought with Victorio. Somehow Bin-daa-dee-nin had managed to keep his family fed by hunting and buying food with silver he stole from somewhere, or so the legend went.

"We've done okay," Mike said aloud. One of his grandmothers was a dealer at the Inn of the Mountain Gods casino, causing a lot of talk in his conservative family. Mike grinned. *Good for Nana*. She was the grandmother related to old Bin-daa-dee-nin. Somehow, from the stories he'd heard, Mike figured Bin-daa-dee-nin would be proud of her.

Tomorrow Mike planned to visit his relatives on the reservation. He might not see them again until the big Fourth of July coming of age ceremony for the Mescalero girls, but there was no way he'd miss that. He didn't want to lose his Apache heritage. *Being clever, whether at Texas Tech or outwitting the U.S. Army, is an Apache trait,* he thought.

The sunlight streamed through the windshield, strong with the promise of spring. Mike relaxed, letting his mind drift from school, to the basketball game, to the yuccas and stumpy mesquite trees dotting the endless tan desert. A gas station, metallic and new against the unchanging landscape, caught his attention.

I want something to drink, he thought, turning the car off the road. *Joe and the high school kids will just have to wait a few minutes more.*

Lindsay tapped her foot and squeezed the gas nozzle harder. The truck always took forever to fill up. Over by the soda machine she saw a guy about her age—or, more accurately, the very attractive back of him, in close-fitting jeans and a tight white T-shirt. *Cute, huh,* she thought. *Hope he turns around.*

Mike punched the Coke button on the soda machine and reached through the slot for his can as it rattled down out of the machine. *Check out those three hot girls in a car,* he thought. *Nice*. He turned around just as Lindsay replaced the gas nozzle on the pump. They both smiled.

Mike heard a commotion from behind the gas station and looked to see what it was.

Lindsay cocked her head and squinted. *What's that noise?* she thought. *It sounds like thunder. But there's not a cloud in the sky.*

A herd of horses burst from behind the gas station, running across the ranchland, their pounding hooves throwing up an enormous cloud of dust. But through it Lindsay could see that the horses were beautiful: palomino and chestnut and even a pair of black-and-white pintos.

She sucked in her breath, almost overpowered by the strange appearance of the horses out of nowhere. For no reason, she imagined herself riding one fast across the hard-packed ground. The image was so vivid, she could almost feel the wind in her hair.

Mike stared at the horses, thinking that they seem to be headed for Cooke's Peak, the tall mountain in the distance—and the gods. *But why should I think that?* he asked himself.

Mike and Lindsay looked at each other at the same time, but this look was different from the first one they exchanged: it was intense and lasting.

Do I know him? Lindsay wondered. *He looks so familiar. . . .*

Mike thought, *That girl's not just cute. Maybe I met her somewhere once. . . .*

TIMELINE OF THE MESCALERO APACHES IN NORTH AMERICA

40,000–13,000 YEARS AGO: Apaches, Eskimos, and other peoples cross from Siberia to Alaska over the Bering Land Bridge. Rising sea levels submerge the bridge. Over time, the Apaches, then called Athabascans, migrate south.

APPROXIMATELY 1500: Apache tribes are driven south into present-day New Mexico and Arizona by the Comanche Indians, a tribe of the southern Great Plains.

1540–1542: The Spanish explorer Francisco Vasquera de Coronado encounters Apaches in eastern Arizona, near the Gila River. One of his companions, Pedro Castañeda, writes in his *Journey of Coronado* that these natives are "barbarous," "live by hunting," and are "intelligent."

1569: The expedition of Don Juan de Oñate encounters Apaches in New Mexico. For the first time the word *Apache* ("enemy") is used for these people. The Spanish divide the Apaches into different groups: the Mescaleros (from the Spanish for "mescal makers," referring to their use of the mescal plant for food) claim lands in New Mexico as far east as Hondo, north to Santa Fe, west to the Rio Grande, and south into Texas. The Jicarillas are in northern and eastern New Mexico and southern Colorado. The Western Apaches roam central and western Arizona. The Chiricahuas live in southern Arizona, down into Sonora and Chihuahua in Mexico.

1600s: The Apaches attack Spanish settlements in Mexico. In 1694 a band of Apaches steal thousands of horses in northern Sonora. The Spanish army pursues the Apaches, killing thirteen of them, but the raiding continues.

1700–1790: Spanish settlements reach almost to the present southern border of the United States. Apache attacks on the settlements worsen. Lieutenant Captain-General Pedro de Labaquera writes to the Spanish king: "The Apaches, when attacked, habitually retired to the mountains, which were inaccessible to the presidial troops. . . . The Apache were wont to get just out of range [of the soldiers' weapons] and make open jest of the Spaniards."

1790–1810: Some groups of Apaches are persuaded to settle down by force and cash support from the Spanish government. In the absence of raids, mines, ranches, and churches flourish in Mexico.

1807: American explorer Zebulon M. Pike is sent from Santa Fe, New Mexico, to Chihuahua, Mexico, to explain to the Spanish government why he trespassed in Spanish territory (at the time the territory in New Mexico belonged to Spain). On the way Pike spots Apaches and writes about their condition and habits.

February 19, 1823: Mexico declares independence from Spain. In the period of confusion and disorganization leading up to and following independence, Apache raids resume. By 1863, the Mexican government offers to pay $100 for every Apache scalp brought in.

1846: The United States declares war on Mexico on May 13, 1846. General Stephen W. Kearny declares himself governor of New Mexico on August 14, 1846. He announces that the U.S. government will protect its citizens from Apache attacks.

February 2, 1848: The United States and Mexico sign the Treaty of Guadalupe Hidalgo. Mexico loses 55 percent of its territory (New Mexico, Arizona, Texas, California, and parts of Colorado, Utah, and Nevada) to the United States.

February 9, 1848: Gold is discovered at Sutter's Mill, near the American River in California. Soon a flood of gold seekers rush across Apache lands in the Southwest.

October 15, 1849: James S. Calhoun, the first Indian agent in New Mexico, writes to the commissioner of Indian Affairs: "The . . . Apaches . . . must be penned up; and this should be done at the earliest possible day."

1854: Fort Davis is built near Limpia Creek in Texas. Over the next twenty years, the Mescaleros attack the fort repeatedly. It is attacked more than any other fort in the country.

April 12, 1861: The American Civil War starts at Fort Sumter, South Carolina. Soldiers at forts in the Southwest are called away to fight back east. The Mescaleros sack Fort Davis, and Apaches lay waste to many mines and settlements.

November 1862: Mescalero Apaches surrender to Kit Carson, soldier and frontiersman, after a fierce battle with soldiers in Dog Canyon, in the Sacramento Mountains of New Mexico. Chief Cadete says, "Do with us as may seem good to you, but do not forget we are men and braves."

March 1863: Over four hundred Mescaleros are taken to a reservation at Bosque Redondo on the Pecos River in New Mexico. About a hundred escape and join Apaches in Mexico.

November 1865: Conditions on the Bosque Redondo reservation are so bad, all the Mescaleros leave, fleeing hunger, disease, and captivity.

February 1870: Mescalero subchief La Paz negotiates with Captain Chambers McKibben, and the Mescaleros go on a new reservation at Fort Stanton, New Mexico. On May 29, 1873, the reservation is officially established by Executive Order of President Ulysses S. Grant.

Fall 1874: A citizen mob massacres sleeping Mescalero men, women, and children on the reservation; surviving Mescaleros flee to the mountains. But soon hunger and cold drive them back to the reservation.

1877: The Fort Stanton reservation is raided and forty of the Mescaleros' horses are stolen; the Mescaleros again leave the reservation. By now, because so many people have moved onto or travel through the Mescaleros' former hunting grounds, game to hunt is scarce. Hungry, some Mescaleros finally return to the reservation, but many don't. Finally, by 1878, the U.S. Army has driven most of them back onto the reservation.

April 1879: Victorio, chief of the Mimbreño Apaches, a branch of the Chiricahuas, leaves the Mescalero reservation when he is told he and his people will be moved to another reservation in San Carlos, Arizona; shortly after, Mescalero chief Caballero leaves the reservation and joins Victorio with two hundred to three hundred people. Pursued by soldiers, the Apaches exist by raiding, crossing and recrossing the U.S.-Mexico border.

September 1879: Victorio returns to Fort Stanton to recruit Apaches still on the reservation.

April 16, 1880: Accused of supplying Victorio's band, the Mescaleros remaining on the reservation are rounded up to be disarmed. Soldiers fire warning shots; the panicked Indians try to escape. Two hundred fifty surrender but many escape and join Victorio. Victorio is now pursued by thousands of U.S. and Mexican soldiers, plus hundreds of cowboys, ranchers, and miners. Victorio's warriors number about 175.

September 1880: Victorio holes up in the Tres Castillos Mountains in Mexico.

October 1880: A group of younger warriors temporarily leave Victorio's band and head north on raids. The warriors skirmish with soldiers in Texas and cannot meet Victorio as planned. Victorio is shot in Tres Castillos, Mexico, by an Indian scout working for the Mexican army. The warriors who escaped are chased throughout the mountains.

1883–1886: Geronimo, a Mimbreño Apache, leads many raids and skirmishes against the U.S. Army. Five thousand U.S. Army troops and five hundred Indian scouts hunt Geronimo; hundreds of Mexican troops and civilians join the chase.

September 3, 1886: Geronimo and his warriors surrender. For four months an army of five thousand has chased Geronimo and thirty-seven Chircahuas. He and all his people, even the scouts who helped the soldiers capture Geronimo, are transported by train to Florida as prisoners of war. A hundred and twelve boys and girls are sent to the Indian School in Carlisle, Pennsylvania, where thirty die.

1913: Surviving members of the exiled Apache groups, numbering only about two hundred, are permitted to settle on the Mescalero reservation in New Mexico.

The present: The Mescalero Apache Tribe numbers about 3,300 and is governed by the ten members of the Mescalero Tribal Council, who are elected by popular vote. The Mescalero reservation is 463,000 acres, much of it mountainous and forest, and many of the tribal government's activities are paid for by timber sales. Almost all Mescaleros speak both Apache and English. They no longer wear buckskin or go on raids but dress like other Americans and work at regular jobs on and off the reservation. Some Mescaleros work at the Inn of the Mountain Gods, an upscale resort and casino, or at Ski Apache, enterprises run by the tribe; others work in the cattle or timber industries or for the government. Tribal traditions are kept alive through education and celebrations, including the annual Fourth of July Mescalero Apache Ceremonial. At the ceremonial a Puberty Ritual Ceremony and a Dance of the Apache Maidens are held for girls, and the Dance of the Mountain Gods is performed to drive away sickness and evil and bring good health and good fortune.

Note on the Apache names: The straight accents in the name Nzhų-'a'c-siin (meaning Keep Ready in Mescalero Apache) are glottal stops—the speaker's breath is interrupted before the syllable that follows the stop. The hook under the *u* means that the symbol is nasal, or uttered with the passage of air through the nose. Bin-daa-dee-nin means Sharp Eyes and Yuu-his-kishn means Colored Beads.